The Miracles
of
Sugar Maple Mountain

by
Edward Love Johnson

Photograph credits:
Maple leaves by Steve Jurvetson.
Walking mountain lion courtesy of the
National Park Service.
Mountain lion head shot by Trisha M. Shears.

CHAPTER I

He came like a fleeting shadow out of the deep dark aisles of the wilderness, his soft pads falling without sound on the hard packed game trail. He paused at the little brook that separated the two worlds to which he claimed private hunting rights. One by grace of birth, the other by choice.

Behind him was the Monongahela, that ruggedly beautiful National Forest that encompassed the towering peaks of the fabled Allegheny Highlands of northeastern West Virginia. It was the land of his birth. A harsh land. A land ruled by the might of the claw and the fang. A land that had schooled him well.

Ahead of him was that other world he had since claimed. That had been almost eight years ago, after a harrowing experience with one of it's residents. That world included the little farming community of Cave Creek Valley and the rugged hills beyond, which the residents called the East Hills, and Sugar Maple Mountain to the west.

THE MIRACLES OF SUGAR MAPLE MOUNTAIN

He was a member of the cat family, a giant of his kind. Out west of the Mississippi he would have been known as a cougar, or perhaps a mountain lion. But to the folks of the eastern highlands he was a panther, and to the residents of that valley he had come to visit, he was Old Crooked Toe. It was a name derived from the track he made in sand or snow with his wounded left rear foot.

His first lesson of life in the wilderness had come at a tender age. As one of a pair of wobbly spotted kittens on their first venture from the sanctity of their lair, he had been attacked by a hunting black bear. Only the swift action of his mother, returning from a hunt, had saved him from the same fate as his sister. That incident had been stored away in his kitten brain. When he came of age, he had made the bears pay.

Many of the black brutes that he encountered over the years were more than double his weight. Yet when the bears discovered, by actual experience, the speed of the panther's forearms, and the knifelike action of his unhooded claws, they gave ground readily.

As Old Crooked Toe paused by the little brook, his amber eyes swept over the western slopes of Sugar Maple Mountain. That was the beginning of his second world, a world he came occasionally to raid, just as the notion suited him.

He lapped a bit of the clear sweet water that splashed down the brook's rocky channel. Then, in typical cat fashion, he crossed the little brook on pebble stones to keep his pads dry. He walked slowly, deliberately, as stately as one would expect the King of the Monongahela to walk.

He padded quietly up the gentle western slope of the mountain, seemingly oblivious to his surroundings. Yet his delicate senses of scent and sound wove for his wily old brain a pattern of life that moved about him. He heard a frightened squirrel race away in dry leaves but he did not bother to look. He knew what it was by the sound. He heard a woodpecker pounding on a hollow dead tree but gave it no notice. It was all a part of life in the great outdoors, but unless it spoke of food or fear, it fostered little attention.

There was a twinge of fall in the air that came down the slope to meet him. Already the leaves had begun to fade and an occasional one fluttered down to dot the forest floor with a bit of color.

At the top of the mountain, Old Crooked Toe paused. He was now on the brink of the gray sandstone cliffs that graced the eastern face of Sugar Maple Mountain. Forty feet straight down they went to a field of great tumbled boulders, fanning out and thinning as they stretched away almost two thirds of the way to the foot of the mountain.

Beyond the boulders, and farther still to the foot of the mountain, were the trees. Great trees. Many of them. They lined the western edge of Cave Creek Valley. Up into the foot of the mountain they came. Trees that had been left when the face of the mountain was timbered. Left because of the sweet water they produced in late winter and on frosty spring mornings. Water that was boiled down to make highly flavored syrups and coarse tasty sugar. It was these sugar maple trees that had given rise to the name of the mountain they now graced.

THE MIRACLES OF SUGAR MAPLE MOUNTAIN

For many minutes Old Crooked Toe stood on the mountain crest, surveying the valley below him. He watched children playing. A dog chased a cat. Cows stood by their feed boxes, waiting for their evening grain and to be milked. There were sheep in the lots. Then there were the farmers wrapping up their work for the day. All a familiar scene. All a part of life in this secluded little valley, peopled by an array of close-knit farm families.

If one had been watching the old panther, they could well have imagined that he was selecting the farm he intended to raid that night. Then again, he could have been looking beyond the valley, all the way across to the East Hills. For that array of wild land that formed the Eastern perimeter of the valley, and climbed up to almost mountain heights, was part of that other territory which the panther claimed as a portion of his vast hunting grounds.

With a singular motion, Old Crooked Toe lifted his great head, opened his mouth and screamed. It was an eerie, ear-splitting call that roiled out across the air in waves. It seemed to bounce off the foothills on either side of the valley and just keep rolling, even echoing in the minds of some who heard it. And everyone who lived in the valley below did hear it.

In the minds of some of them, it was the call of a mystical old creature, one who had survived dozens of plots to kill him over the past eight years. They welcomed his visits, believing him to possess some sort of psychic powers that had been instrumental in keeping him alive.

To those who had suffered livestock losses, it was a different story. He was a scourge, an evil old Devil who deserved to die. To that end, they had expended every means known. Nothing had worked. More than a half dozen dogs had died from the poisoned meats which the old panther refused to touch. Every known type of trap or deadfall was cleverly avoided.

Great hunting parties scoured the back slopes of Sugar Maple Mountain and deep into the vast reaches of the Monongahela. They always came up blank. Every type of hunting dog had been brought in on the hunt, including the plot hound. Even those short legged, heavy bodied dogs, bred as bear fighters, were no match for the speed and agility of the panther.

Still, Old Crooked Toe came. He came sporadically, never on a predictable schedule. There was only one thing could the residents of the valley be certain of. He always brazenly announced his presence with each visit. And it was always a call sufficiently loud for all to hear.

Today, as he did on most visits, the panther retreated into the deep woods on the back slopes. He found a dense thicket and curled up to comfortably wait for the cover of darkness. Again, as on most occasions, he would not leave the mountain top until midnight had passed, life in the valley had completely quieted, and the silvery rim of a new moon hung like a jewel over the crest of the East Hills.

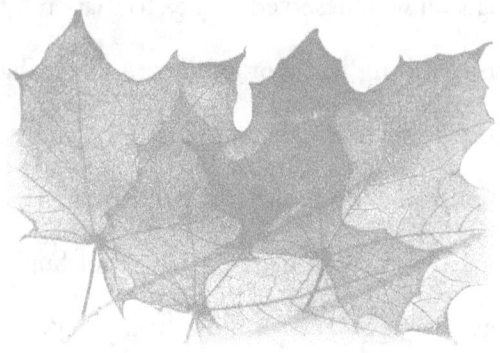

CHAPTER 2

Kennie Reeves was unhitching his team when he heard the scream. He jerked erect. Unconsciously his hand went up to grab the brass knob atop the hame of the harness on Prince, the big bay gelding that was the lead horse of his team. He leaned against the horse and felt him trembling. He put his arm about Prince's neck and spoke to him softly. Just as he had spoken to him on that dark and frightening night there on the back slopes of Sugar Maple Mountain. Almost eight years had passed since that experience, yet there lingered an association between the horse, the man, the brass knob and the panther that had just announced his presence to residents of Cave Creek Valley.

Whatever that association was, it had been a well-kept secret for all of those eight years. But that was just one of the many secrets that shrouded the deep recesses of Sugar Maple Mountain. Some were destined to eventually be revealed, some to remain locked away in their respective enclave.

Although the caller was close to a mile away, Kennie knew that he was atop the jagged sandstone cliffs that rimmed the southern crest of Sugar Maple Mountain. That was where he had announced his presence on previous occasions when he had come to raid the farms of Cave Creek Valley. That was where his trail always ended when he vanished like a shadow back into the mythical wilds of the Monongahela.

Kennie stood for several minutes, listening for a second call. When no call came, he finished unhitching the team and led it hastily to the log barn beside the sheep lot. He skinned off the harness and watered them. Then, with a gentle pat, he sent each horse back to his stall where a generous helping of grain and hay awaited them.

As he reached the house, Kennie paused, his hand on the doorknob. He was thinking, fighting in his mind for a way, should the opportunity arise, to once again avoid killing the big cat.

Why did Old Crooked Toe (it was Kennie who had first named the panther long ago) keep coming back? Why didn't he keep to his secret retreats far back in the wilds of that Great National Forest?

And now, once again, everyone would be asking Kennie the same question. "Do you really want to kill that panther?"

Nancy Reeves was forking thick slices of fried ham from an iron skillet onto a serving tray when Kennie entered the kitchen. She turned to face him, peering over the top of horn-rimmed glasses. He knew what was coming.

"Did you hear that?" Nancy said.

"Hear what?" Kennie replied, trying to sound casual as he took off his cap and jacket and threw them onto a nearby chair.

" 'Hear what?' You know what. That big killer cat you call Old Crooked Toe. I was inside and I heard him. So I'm sure you heard him when you were outside."

"Oh. Yes, Mom. It did sound like Old Crooked Toe, didn't it?"

"You got the sheep locked in the barn?"

"No. But I do have them in the back lot."

"Then you'll be missing a lamb or maybe one of your prize ewes come morning."

"Maybe, and then maybe not." Kennie said. "He is now most a mile away. Take him a while to get here. Could be, one or two of those fancy hounds some of the farmers have been importing will chase him back to where he came from. At least I can hope they do."

"Why did you work so late?" Nancy asked. "Did you forget that you told Katie you'd see her tonight?"

"No, I didn't forget. Well, maybe for just a little bit. But I wanted to get my field ready to plant tomorrow. I'm sure she'll understand."

"Wash up and let's get to this food while it's hot," Nancy said.

Kennie and Nancy had hardly seated themselves at the table and begun loading their plates with ham, baked beans and apple sauce, when someone knocked on the door.

Kennie half turned in his chair.

"Come in," he said.

The door opened slowly. Crippled old Pete Higgins, from across the valley, hobbled in.

"Just dropped by to see if you'd heard that darned old cat scream," he said.

Kennie smiled. "You mean, Pete, that you've hobbled all the way across the valley since Old Crooked Toe announced his presence?"

"Well, I was about halfway here when I heard that cat," Pete chuckled. "I must admit, I remembered Monday night was ham and beans night. There's nobody else can match your mom's ham and beans!"

Nancy looked at Pete's humped back and his twisted leg. Pete had saved the Lee girl from a speeding car all those years ago. But it had cost him.

Now, somehow, she was associating him with her son and the cat, but she didn't know just how.

"Thanks Pete," she said softly. "I'm glad you enjoy my cooking. It's always good to have you with us. I baked those beans just the way you like them."

"Grab a plate there at the end of the table," Kennie said. "You know where the forks are. So drag up a chair and dig in".

"Not much of a cook myself," Pete said as he began to load his plate. "Fact is, I ain't no cook at all. Molly was a good cook. But in these long years since she passed I just haven't learned myself very much about cooking. Maybe I haven't tried very hard."

Pete loaded his plate and busied himself with his fork for a while. Then he turned to Kennie.

"When you gonna kill that big cat?" he asked. "You're the only farmer hereabouts who's young enough to take up a rifle and really go after that scamp."

Kennie had expected that one. The fact was, he would get the same question from his mother before the night was over. He placed his knife and fork on his plate and leaned back in his chair.

"I'll be asked that question several times in the next few days," he said. "Everybody knows that the Monongahela is a big place, that is, until they want me to go in there and run that Panther to earth. Then suddenly that big forest shrinks down to just a common old woodland."

"But what about when he's out here in the open?" Pete asked. "And let me tell you what I've been doing. I've been working on a big live animal trap which might just nail that old rascal."

"You have had some big ideas before," Kennie chuckled. "Remember the chicken coop where the chicken could let itself in and out? Or that back-scratcher for your dog that you tried to get patented?"

Pete smiled. "Yes, and a half dozen others that didn't make sense," he said. "But this trap, it just might work. I've been working on it since the last time Old Crooked Toe was here."

"You know, Pete," Kennie said, "there are several folks here in the valley that don't want that old panther killed, especially since he run off that interloper."

"I know," Pete replied. "But not me."

Pete put away another helping of baked beans. Soon he turned to Kennie again.

"There's another thing I've been wanting to ask you, Kennie," Pete said.

"Well," Kennie said, "since you're so full of questions, go ahead."

" Just when are you and Miss Katie Bonner going to get hitched?" Pete asked.

"We haven't had a wedding in the valley for quite a spell," Nancy chimed in.

"I know you have your mom to care for and Katie has her Dad," Pete said, "but you shouldn't let that stop you."

"Don't you think that's a bit personal Pete?" Kennie smiled. "Besides, if I did tell you, everybody in the valley would know it by tomorrow night."

"Nancy, did you hear what that son of yours just said to me?" Pete asked. "Makes me think he hasn't got no faith in me at all."

"He must be kidding," Nancy mused. "Maybe that's why he hasn't told me."

After Pete left, Kennie went into the living room and called Katie.

"I'm sorry to be calling so late," he said. "Pete came over. You know how that goes."

"Yes," Katie sighed. "It's the same thing over here on Wednesday night, when he comes over for Mom's chicken dumplings."

"I had to work late, too. I was trying to get my field ready to plant wheat tomorrow. And you know what else has happened."

"Yes, I'm certain everybody in the valley heard," Katie said. "You know how upset Daddy gets when Old Crooked Toe comes calling."

"I'd bet it's been much worse since that big rascal made off with his prize pig," said Kennie.

"That's true," Katie said, "He's in such a foul mood, maybe it's best you don't come over tonight. We can talk tomorrow after I get home from work."

CHAPTER 3

L ater during the night, Nancy heard the kitchen door open and close quietly. Close to half an hour later, she heard the door open and shut again. She went back to sleep.

Later, she was awakened a second time by the sound of the kitchen door opening and closing. This time she got up and watched, from the kitchen window, the shadowy form of her son meander up past the corner of the barn and around to the sheep lot.

But on this second trip it seemed less than ten minutes until she saw him returning. She slipped quietly back into bed before her son saw her watching, but she did not go back to sleep. The mystery of the relationship between her son and that old panther just seemed to continue to grow. There were no answers, just more questions.

Kennie did not have to tell Nancy what had happened in the sheep lot during the night. His mother had insisted on accompanying him to check the sheep the next morning.

When they reached the lot they began the count. All of his prime ewes were there. Kennie had used great care in selecting his best ewes for his breeding stock. That way he had built up a very good and highly productive flock. He fed his sheep every day, year around. That meant he was working with them every day. That made for a good relationship when lambing season came during the bitter winter.

Then they counted the lambs. One was missing. They counted again. There was no wool, no blood, just one lamb absent from the flock.

Apparently, some predator had been here. One big enough to carry away his kill. And Nancy and Kennie both had an opinion as to who had enjoyed a dinner of mutton somewhere far back in the deep recesses of Sugar Maple Mountain.

Nancy didn't say," I told you so." Instead, she said softly, "Maybe we had best lock them in the barn tonight."

She got no reply. Instead, her son stood silent, his forearm on the top plank of the fence, his chin resting on his arm.

He was not looking at the sheep. He was not looking at the gate, still closed and latched. He was looking out across the valley, out to the deep woods where the panther might be at that moment.

This same thing had happened before. That had been the first time the old panther came calling on the valley. Kennie had lost a sheep to the big cat. He had passed up all the other farms and had come close to a mile into the valley, to settle on Kennie's place to make his kill.

Today, as on that previous occasion, Kennie showed no anger toward the presumed predator. So, again, the question popped into Nancy's mind -- What was the relationship between her son and Old Crooked Toe? She would never ask Kennie.

In fact, that question went all the way back to that frightful night almost eight years ago, the night when the faithful old horse had brought Kennie to the back porch with a broken leg. He was in a terrible state of shock. In the days following, she often thought that Kennie had not told all that happened that night.

As the years went by, Nancy had come to feel that there was some mysterious relationship between her son and the panther. Today, she was certain.

"I'm going back to the house and make us some breakfast," Nancy said. "You come on in when you are ready."

Back in the house, Nancy watched her son from the kitchen window. He had not moved.

As Nancy stood watching her son, her thoughts went back to seven years ago, when her husband Sidney had died.

She had watched helplessly as Sidney reared up in bed. She saw Kennie place his arm around his father's shoulders and hold him.

"Promise me that you will take care of your mother for as long as she lives," Sidney had said.

"I promise," Kennie sobbed.

Sidney slumped in his son's arms. He was gone.

Over the years, that promise had become a great concern to Nancy. She did not want her son tied down because of it. On several occasions she had talked to Kennie, trying to emphasize that she wanted him to have a life of his own.

She realized the relationship between Kennie and Katie Bonner was serious. She had the feeling that the promise Kennie had made his Dad was keeping them apart. And it bothered her -- bothered her a lot.

Kennie planted his wheat the next day. He had his seed and ground ready when Elliot Conner came about mid-morning with his team and drill. By noon they had the planting done. Nancy invited Elliot to stay for lunch, but he declined. He wanted to get along, since he had promised Bill Little to plant his wheat that afternoon.

Cave Creek, which wound it's erratic course down through the valley, got it's headwaters from the mouth of a cave at the southern end of the mountain. As the stream flowed down the valley it was fed by various springs along the foot of the mountain, becoming a rather strong stream before it reached Chrystal River just beyond the north end of the mountain.

It was one of those little branches of Cave Creek that Kennie followed in the afternoon. He was looking for further evidence of what had happened to the lamb that had disappeared last night.

About a third of the way up the mountain, Kennie came to a small level bench winding it's way in and out of the valley and around the ridge. He followed the bench a considerable distance. Just as he was about to give up, he found what he was looking for. On the upper side of the bench, almost hidden by a clump of maple leaf viburnum, was the lamb's head, some scattered bits of wool, and a few bones.

Kennie stood staring at the remains, incidents from the past racing through his mind. Then, he stirred, as if coming out of a trance. He kicked leaves over the remains, shouldered his rifle and turned wearily homeward.

It was early in the evening when Katie called. Her Dad had called her at work. He had some news that he wanted Kennie to know about, but he didn't have time to talk just then. He said that he would tell her about it when he got home. Katie said she would come over to see Kennie as soon as she talked to her Dad.

Kennie did his feeding early. When Katie came, they went into the living room and had coffee and sweet rolls.

"Daddy says some of the residents are making plans for a big hunt," she said. "He was down at the service station this morning and heard them talking about it. The Beeler brothers, Tom and Jerry, have a couple of new hounds. They say that they're experienced cat dogs. They think they'll run Old Crooked Toe to earth this time."

"Aren't those the fellows who brought in the greyhound?" Kennie asked. "Do you remember what happened to it?"

Katie did remember. The Beelers were certain the greyhound could outrun the panther, and it did. However, the greyhound had been accustomed to running up beside it's racing partner, so when it ran up beside the panther, the cat took a swipe at its side. The hound let out a yelp and headed out of the south end of the valley at his very best pace. The Beelers were so disgusted with the dog's performance that when he didn't come back, they never went looking for him, even though they had paid a pretty fair price for him.

"So, how does this big hunt involve me?" Kennie asked.

"They want you to join the hunt. Tom Beeler said you wouldn't. He said you didn't really want to kill the Panther," Katie said. She paused.

"And you want to know my thinking?" she asked. "I have, at times, thought they might be right. But I'll never ask you why."

Kennie looked long at Katie. The question had been presented verbally, but he was reading a more direct question in her expression, and that was the one that bothered him.

"I see," Kennie said. "Well, there is something that I have never told anyone, not even Mom. And yes, it does involve the Panther. If and when I do decide to make it known, you'll be the first to hear. As for going on the hunt with them, of course I will, if they ask me."

Katie was silent for a bit.

"Daddy said they plan to catch Old Crooked Toe when he is in the hills on the east side of the valley and put the hounds on his trail. That way they hope to tree him before he can get across the valley and up into those rugged cliffs on the south end of the mountain."

"And just how do they expect to know when the Panther is in the East Hills?" Kennie asked.

Katie smiled. "Dad thought that was a good question, too. It seemed that everyone had a different solution. They finally agreed to report it to Sam Landers at the gas station, and Sam would get the word out to the hunters. Then they would meet near the sighting, and go on from there. Dad wasn't sure any of them knew what they were doing."

"Those hills over east of the valley have all been timbered rather heavy in recent years." Kennie said. "There isn't a tree big enough for a cat of that size to climb. From what my dad told me about his experiences with big cats, with just two hounds on his tail, Old Crooked Toe would turn and fight before he would try to shinny up one of those saplings."

Katie said, "Dad said some of the others were bringing dogs."

"I have an idea," Kennie said. "Suppose you get your Dad. Mom and I will meet you over at Joe's Place. We can have a sandwich or something. That way neither you nor Mom will have to cook this evening. Then we can talk about this great venture that the Cave Creek Valley folks are planning.

"What if Pete comes about the time you are ready to leave?" she asked.

"I'll just bring him along," Kennie said.

"It's a deal!" Katie said. "See you later." And she was gone.

…..

Pete did show up, just as Kennie and Nancy were leaving. So they loaded him in the back seat and took him with them.

It had been a long time since Pete had been out to eat, so it promised to be a real experience for him. Kennie pulled two tables close so they could all sit together. They were the only patrons present at the time, and Pete leaned close to Katie and whispered, "How can Joe afford to hire all these young girls I see here?"

"They're not employees," Katie said. "They're high school girls that hang out here -- Just to be around Joe. They all fall for his dark brown eyes and black hair. They help him with the tables just to be near him. When he closes he usually treats them to a dip of ice cream."

When the waitress came to take their orders, everyone placed an order except Pete. He gave a wistful look at the menu and passed it back to the waitress.

"Just give me a biscuit with a slice of ham on it," Pete said. "And put some of that other stuff on it like you're putting on Kennie's sandwich."

CHAPTER 4

It was two days before Bill Little called Kennie about the hunt. "When I was a young man," Bill said, "we would occasionally do some night hunting. The weather had to be right, but there were always just two or three of us. Hunting with a big crowd doesn't make much sense to me."

Still, Bill invited Kennie to join the hunt, and Kennie said to count him in.

Things were quiet for a few days, then there were two sightings in rapid succession. In the first case both of the Beeler brothers came and brought their two hounds.

They covered the entire area around the reported sighting, but the hounds could not pick up a cat scent. While they were putting the dogs back in the truck, they heard a series of yips and howls. A large Beagle broke out of the brush hot on the trail of a rabbit.

The second sighting turned out to be the same dog.

The next day, the widow Boone reported a beige animal in the brush on the hill behind her place. A neighbor who had been scanning the hills with a pair of binoculars also saw movement. Both of them told Sam Landers at the service station that the animal was too large to be a dog.

Jerry Beeler brought one of the hounds over on a leash to see if it could pick up a trail. If he could pick up a scent, the other hounds would be brought out as well.

Yet again hopes were dashed.

The culprit was the widow Boone's Jersey cow. She had broken out of the pasture and was enjoying a bit of adventure. But that operation was not a complete loss. The hunters rounded up the errant cow, got her back in the pasture, and repaired the widow Boone's fence.

Then there was a lull in reported sightings, but only briefly. It appeared that Old Crooked Toe wanted to teach the Beeler brothers and their new hounds a lesson. Without his usual announcement, he had slipped quietly into the valley and took up residence in the East Hills.

On a quiet Sunday night, with just a hint of frost in the air, and under a full moon, the Panther struck again. He slipped into Jerry Beeler's back pasture where he struck down a four-month-old calf. His attack was almost within sight of the two chained hounds. He stuffed himself to contentment and slipped back into the brushy slopes of the East Hills.

So the call went out on a cool Monday morning. Would-be hunters began to gather, some up at the Beeler place and some at the service station.

Kennie was still doing his chores when he heard about the attack. He finished his milking and took time to eat breakfast. He knew that Old Crooked Toe was a long time gone from the place of his kill.

After breakfast he picked up Pete at his place, and they went to the service station. Soon more hunters showed up. Their plan was to spread out down the valley to head off the old Panther in case he attempted to cross the valley to Sugar Maple Mountain.

Before long the Beeler hounds were singing their trail song, a sound that is sweet music to the ears of hound dog men. The hounds swept down the East Hills, their voices fading as they dipped down into the valleys, then coming on strong as they climbed back up to high ground again.

The hounds had almost reached the hills in back of the service station when the singing became erratic.

"He has pulled one of his tricks," Bill Little said.

"How has he done that?" Jerry Beeler asked.

"When he is well ahead of the hounds," Bill explained. "He turns back on his own trail for forty or fifty feet. He then leaps far to either the right or left and heads straight away from his original trail. The hounds overshoot the trail for several feet before they realize they have lost the scent. They will then swing wide in a circle to find the scent again."

"Do you think he will head this way?" Jerry asked.

"Probably not," Bill said. "We'll soon know. If I was guessing I would say he will head up the hill."

Abruptly the baying turned to normal and headed straight up the back of the ridge directly above the station.

"I hope they're not heading to those rugged mountains to the northeast," Cory Long, who had now joined the gathering crowd, said.

"They are not going that way," Bill said. "They'll turn south, back toward Jerry's place."

Just as Bill had predicted, there was a break again in the routine baying of the hounds. When they had the trail unravelled, they were headed back toward Jerry's place.

"How'd you guess what that panther would do?" Jerry asked.

"I wasn't guessing," Bill said. "Old Crooked Toe was just following the same pattern he used the time he killed Walter's dog."

"How did he kill your dog?" Jerry asked Walter Bland who had now joined the crowd.

"Just like Bill said. Old Crooked Toe pulled the same trick on my dog. That gave him a good lead by the time he got to the upper end of the valley. So he crossed into the mountain and headed for the cliffs there on the mountain top.

"Down on the face of that cliff, the old panther has a secret cove of some sort. You can't get to it," Walter said.

"The path down to the cove is just a break in the rock," Bill said. "It's so narrow and rugged you'd wonder how an animal the size of Old Croaked Toe could navigate it, but he does."

"Most dogs would never venture out on that narrow outcrop, but my dog did," Walter continued. "And the old panther swept him off of the cliff when he reached the cove.

"I could have held him, but I never dreamed that he would tackle such a narrow, rugged path. After he fell, I climbed down and worked my way out through those tumbled boulders at the cliff base. He was already dead when I got there. He had landed on one of the boulders and fractured his skull."

Jerry turned to Tom. "We'd better get out there fast," he said. "We don't want to lose another dog." They jumped in their car and drove rapidly across the valley and up the old skid road as far as it was safe to go. Then they got out and started climbing fast.

"I hope they make it," Walter said.

By now residents on the eastern side of the creek had begun to appear up and down the foothills, racing along as though they were hoping to cut off the panther. As the course of the hounds changed, they all paused.

No one knew which way to go. And that certainly would have been in Old Crooked Toe's best interest, if he had wanted to cross the valley.

But he didn't want to cross the valley.

Already he had reached the Beeler farms. He turned and, passing through Jerry Beeler's yard, ran within sight of Tom Beeler's house with impunity. Then he headed for the rugged cliffs that everyone had hoped to keep him from reaching.

Kennie loaded Bill Little, Elliot Conner and Cory Long in his car and crossed the valley to the skid road, where everyone was gathering. There was already a discussion going on about just who should go up after the cat, and who should not.

Kennie, the youngest in the group, suggested that Elliot Conner, Bill Little, Cory Long and himself go. With the two Beelers that would make six. Yet old Ralph Billups, who had limped all the way across the valley, insisted that he go, too.

"You have already had two heart attacks," Kennie protested. "That's a pretty steep climb, Ralph. Don't you think that might be too much for you?"

"I'll make it," Ralph insisted. "And don't you forget young man, I was chasing them critters long before you were born. You'll need my advice and help up there."

To prove his expertise, Ralph had brought along a rope.

Once they were on top of the mountain, the group checked the cliff rim in both directions from the ledge where Old Crooked Toe had sought shelter.

"Maybe there's a point where we can see back into the old panther's cave." Ralph said.

And, sure enough, they found a point about thirty feet to the north where there was a protrusion on the face of the cliff. It was about ten feet down and had sufficient room on the base of the protrusion for a man to stand. Yet reaching it would be a difficult and extremely dangerous venture.

Bill Little took a dim view of the idea.

"You can't see back into that cove," he said. "It's just plain dangerous. That cliff must be at least forty feet high."

Ralph, who had taken it upon himself to be boss, contended that he knew how to get down to the cove.

What Ralph wanted was a volunteer. He would tie the rope securely about the man's waist, and the other end to a tree, leaving sufficient slack to reach the outcrop. Then three or four men would get on the rope and let the slack out as the volunteer needed it.

"It can be safely done," Ralph insisted. "I bet it will give a good shot back into the panther's cove"

In the meantime, another group of old-timers, some of whom really had no business on the mountain top, had joined the group of onlookers.

"It's a crowd," Bill Little said to Kennie. "I don't like it. Some of these fellows need caretakers themselves. We may have to appoint someone to keep them back from the edge of the cliff."

Ralph was having trouble getting a volunteer. Three men had come forward, taken one look at the cliff face and backed off, shaking their heads.

When no one would volunteer, Ralph approached Kennie.

"Just take a look here," he insisted. "It isn't as dangerous as some keep making it out."

"Is that a good rope?" Kennie asked.

When Ralph insisted that the rope was safe, Kennie finally agreed to be lowered to the ledge and see if he could get a look at the Panther.

Ralph secured the rope tight about Kennie's middle and tied off the other end to a nearby tree, leaving the rope slack.

When it seemed that everything was in proper order, Bill Little, Cory Long and Elliot Conner joined Ralph on the rope. Very slowly, they eased out the rope as Kennie worked his way down.

They got him to the ledge and were holding tight until he could get his feet firmly planted on the narrow outcrop. That was when Bill Little felt the rope behind him go slack. He turned his head in time to see Ralph straighten up and fall over backwards.

Bill yelled for help. Both of the Beeler brothers put their hounds on leash and tied them to a tree and came running. Tom took over Ralph's place on the rope and Jerry got down close to the edge of the cliff.

"We have a problem up here with Ralph," Bill called down to Kennie. "We want to get you back up, so start climbing. We'll keep the rope taut."

When Kennie tried to climb, he found few hand holds deep enough to help him. On the way down there had been some traction from the rough face of the cliff wall, but that was no help climbing up.

Jerry, who was closest to the cliff, could see what was happening.

"We'll have to drag him up," Jerry said. "Slow and easy! Let's all pull together."

When they had Kennie about halfway up, Jerry noticed that the rope was fraying as it rubbed over the sharp edge of the cliff rim.

"Hold it," he shouted. "We've got to get a shimmy of some kind between the rope and the cliff edge. We don't want the rope to break! Does anyone have anything that might work as a cushion?"

"My cap has a leather bill," Cory said. "It's a new cap so it should be strong enough."

"Let's try it!" Jerry said.

Cory passed his cap down. Jerry placed the cap bill just below the rock edge and held it there while they gave the rope a slight pull. It didn't work. With Kennie's weight on the rope, the cap bill wouldn't slide under the rope.

"We'll have to let him back down and get some slack on the rope so I can get the cap bill under it." Jerry said. "So, very slowly, ease him back down."

While all of this was going on the crowd stood mesmerized. No one spoke. No one moved. The only movement came as even more townspeople came up the hill to watch the show.

Among these late-comers were Susan Lee and Katie Bonner. They both worked at the bank just beyond the upper end of the valley. They were returning from work when they saw the mass of parked cars and pick-ups at the base of the mountain. They had pulled over and joined the crowd climbing up the mountain to witness the action.

"Who is down there?" Katie asked.

Someone told her it was Kennie Reeves. Katie exploded. She screamed and ran toward the cliff face. Susan grabbed her arm, but was losing her grip. Lemuel

Long, who had also just arrived, grabbed Katie around the waist and held her fast.

"Hold on there, Katie," he said, trying to calm her. "You'd just be in the way!" Together Susan and Lemuel finally calmed her down.

"Those fellows working the rope have their hands full without you adding to their problems," Susan said.

Still crying, Katie clung to Susan. Fortunately for her, she did not know how bad Kennie's situation actually was, that Kennie was about halfway down the cliff face, dangling at the end of a fraying rope.

At Jerry's direction the men on the rope began to ease Kennie back down. When he reached the ledge they gave Jerry enough slack on the rope so he could slide the cap bill in between the rope and the sharp edge of the Cliff face.

"Pull easy," Jerry said. "I'm going to try to hold the cap bill in place with my hands. If it starts slipping I'll holler."

Once again they hauled Kennie up. It went well until they were trying to pull him over the edge of the cliff. The knotted rope on Kennie's middle hung up at the corner of the cliff face, and they couldn't pull it any further.

Jerry called for help and Bill Little got one of the onlookers to take his place on the pull. He ran down to the other side of the rope from Jerry. Working together, the two of them were able to get the knotted rope up over the edge.

"Now pull," Jerry said to the men on the rope. They gave a heave.

That was when the rope broke. Katie screamed as Lemuel dived down on the ground between Jerry and Bill Little.

Without Lemuel's help, Susan could barely hold onto Katie.

Lemuel grabbed one of Kennie's arms with both hands.

Kennie finally found a toe hold on the cliff face and gave a lurch. With the help of the three holding him, he scrambled to safety.

Bill leaped up, grabbed Kennie and pulled him well away from the cliff edge. His face was white and his hands were trembling so hard that he had trouble getting the rope untied from around Kennie's waist. When he finally succeeded he threw the rope out over the cliff as far as he could.

"Thank God you're safe!" he said. "We'll never try that again, not if I have anything to do with it."

When Susan saw Kennie was safe and well away from the edge of the cliff, she released Katie, who ran to Kennie and threw her arms around him.

Both of the Beeler brothers had experience in the medical field. Tom had been a massage therapist. Jerry had served with the medics while in the military. After release from the Army he had worked in an Emergency Room for many years before he retired and moved into the valley. They turned their attention to Ralph, checking vitals and doing what they could on the mountain top to stabilize the patient. Then they called for volunteers to give up their jackets to be used in tying together a makeshift stretcher.

In what seemed like a very few short minutes, they had their patient ready to be carried off of the Mountain, and there were plenty of volunteers to help with the carry.

All of those watching the ease with which the brothers worked over their patient instantly had a new respect for them. Thus the two Beeler brothers, who had found some problem fitting into the community, were suddenly a new part of the valley culture.

While the Beelers attended to Ralph, Susan Lee ran down the mountain to get to a phone and call an ambulance.

In the meantime, the Beelers readied their patient for his trip down the mountain. Jerry Beeler would attend the patient. Tom ran to get the hounds and drag them away from the quarry that they did not want to leave.

With a makeshift stretcher tied together, Jerry placed two men on either side of Ralph, Kennie out front holding his legs, and a sixth man on his head. They began the long trek down the mountain. By the time they reached the foot of the skid road, an ambulance was already coming toward them with lights flashing and siren blaring.

Katie had walked beside Kennie all the way down. She had finally gotten control of her emotions.

When they had Ralph loaded and the ambulance on the way, everyone breathed a sigh of relief. For a few minutes some of them paused, expressing fright, disappointment and near disbelief.

Tom Beeler was getting into his car and Jerry was standing on the passenger side with his hand on the door when he turned to Kennie.

"When that rope began to fray," he said, "I realized that you were dangling there on an old and rotten rope. To say I was frightened doesn't begin to tell you how I really felt. What I want you to know is, at that point I began silently talking to God, very seriously, and I'm convinced He heard me. Otherwise you wouldn't be standing here, listening to me."

Jerry stepped into the car and the Beeler brothers drove away, leaving Kennie in shock. He hadn't fully realized what was going on when it had taken Jerry and the others so long to get him up. He stood silently for a moment, letting Jerry's words sink in. Then he turned to Bill Little and suggested that they should be on their way home. They loaded up without further conversation.

Kennie drove Bill, Cory and Elliot home. Then he swung by the service station to pick up Pete.

News of the harrowing experience had reached the station well before Kennie got there and he found Pete livid. The crippled old man had trouble finding words to express his disdain that Kennie had agreed to take such a dangerous risk, and he continued after they were in the car.

To slow things down, Kennie reminded Pete that this was Monday and that if he would stay for dinner he would drive him home later. That helped briefly, yet when Pete and Nancy got together they really laid it on. That was when Kennie decided it was time to get out and do his chores, and why he found some extra tasks that took him considerably longer than usual. He didn't go in until his Mother called to tell him dinner was ready.

After dinner Kennie drove Pete home. At Pete's insistence, they went out to the barn to have a look at the trap. It was a rather monstrous thing and almost completed. "Just another day or two and I'll be ready for Old Crooked Toe," Pete said. "And let me tell you something. Old Crooked Toe is going to be in there before the year is over."

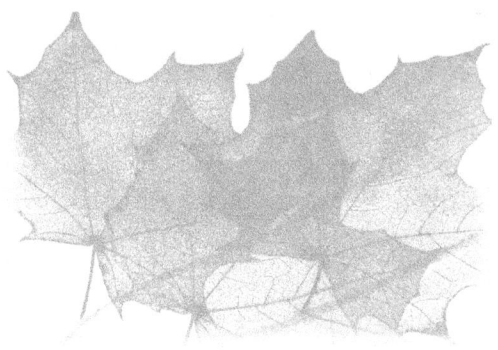

CHAPTER 5

The gravity of Kennie's experience did not hit him fully until he went to bed that night. As he replayed Jerry's words, and considered what might well have happened on the cliff top, he found it impossible to go to sleep.

Then his thoughts went once again to that other frightful day now almost eight years ago. Was this another miracle? Certainly that other was. It seemed there was a connection. Both involved the old panther. Maybe in graphically different ways, but still the old panther was the focal character. He was that other day long ago. He was again today.

When three hours had passed without sleep, Kennie got out of bed. He pulled the hidden evidence of that other experience out from under the bed. He unwrapped it, studied it briefly, then rewrapped it securely and slid it back into hiding.

This was something he had done many times over the years. He always found some solace in the evidence of what Old Crooked Toe had done that other fateful day. Then he got down on his knees beside the bed and thanked God once again for His great blessings, both of this day and on that other day.

Before Kennie dozed off, he had another thought. Now there was a new secret hidden away atop Sugar Maple Mountain. For no one had bothered to ask him if he had been able to see into Old Crooked Toe's secret cove in the few minutes that he had been on the ledge. Nor had he bothered to tell them that he had.

In fact, he had seen the old panther laying there on the ledge with his head cradled on his outstretched paws, seemingly oblivious to the commotion that was going on just a few feet above him.

On the following day there was much speculation about what might have happened to Old Crooked Toe. Most believed the old panther was once again well hidden somewhere back in the secret coves and mysterious dales of the Monongahela.

There was some suggestion that the Beelers should put their hounds on the trail of Old Crooked Toe and see what happened after everyone cleared the mountain top, but they refused, afraid the coy old marauder might lead the dogs so deep in the forest that they would never find their way home. So the mystery of when and where Old Crooked Toe went, remained just that -- a mystery.

The great panther chase totally dominated the talk of the community for quite a long time. Not surprisingly the story didn't shrink. Rather it seemed to grow with each retelling. Some of it was news even to Kennie, who listened quietly, and spoke little.

The excitement of the chase did many things. For one, it got Pete in gear. In little more than a week he hobbled across the valley to inform Kennie that he was ready for the old panther's next visit.

He wanted Kennie to help him get the trap moved over to the sheep lot in back of Kennie's barn. "That's where the critter made his first kill," Pete reckoned. "And he seems to be a creature of habit."

For the next two weeks Kennie busied himself with farm work. Yet something kept bothering him. He asked himself the same question over and over again. Could he have really pulled the trigger on the rifle there on the ledge if he had had Old Crooked Toe in his sights?

So it was that on a bright Fall day, Kennie took his rifle, crossed the valley, and hit the deep woods. He had the day before him so he moved leisurely, enjoying the sweetness of the fall forest. Hearing the twitter of migrating birds and seeing them flit away at his approach. Watching the bright red and gold leaves float downward on the gentle breeze. Enjoying the sweet earthy odors that came so freely with the changing of the seasons.

He climbed up the face of Sugar Maple Mountain, down its back slopes and buried himself in the fastness of the always changing, always mystical Monongahela. He had walked farther into the sprawling forest than usual when he found a little spring. It's clear, cool waters bubbled out from beneath a rock ledge at the foot of a steep incline. It seemed so inviting that he decided to eat the sandwich he had tucked away in his back pack.

After he finished his sandwich, Kennie dropped down and drank from the sweet, clear waters of the spring. He then decided to go just a little farther before he turned homeward. That was when he heard a commotion out ahead. It was the birds. They were twittering loudly, scolding something, or someone. Kennie took the rifle from his shoulder and placed his finger on the trigger.

Then he came, around a bend in the trail, walking slowly, deliberately, like the king of the Monongahela that he was, Old Crooked Toe.

The old panther did not leap from the trail and race away as one might have expected him to do. Instead he paused and for long moments the eyes of the two met, just as they had met on that fateful night almost eight years ago. Some message seemed to pass between them, maybe friendship, maybe understanding. Only God knew.

Then, as slowly and deliberately as he had come, he went. Turning, he disappeared around the bend in the trail. Kennie was left standing alone, his finger still on the trigger. What he had learned in those brief moments, he already knew. Without others watching, expecting, he could not pull that trigger, not while looking eye to eye. He lowered the rifle, placed it back on his shoulder and turned homeward.

If anyone had gotten the idea that Old Crooked Toe was frightened by the great hound chase, they were wrong. It was slightly more than a month before he announced his presence again. And yes, once again he came from the top of the cliffs where he had sheltered from the great chase -- That monumental event that was still embedded in the minds of many of the residents of Cave Creek Valley. That monumental event that had come so near to ending in a monumental disaster.

The panther's call had come a bit earlier in the evening than usual. To most, it seemed a bit more forceful, even frightening. Yet to crippled old Pete Higgins it was sweet music. It brought a picture to his mind of the old panther lashing out at the iron bars that were designed to keep him in confinement until he could be put away. And to Pete's delight, it was Monday — ham and baked beans at the Reeves household. So he had a two-fold purpose in hobbling across the valley to the Reeves residence.

Kennie was stashing a wagon load of second cutting hay in the barn loft when Pete arrived.

"What brings you here at this early hour?" Kennie asked, a broad grin on his face. "It won't be dinner time for a couple hours yet."

"You know what brings me here."

"Oh," Kennie said. "I did hear something. Do you think that was really Old Crooked Toe this early in the evening?"

"Of course it was that old rascal," Pete said. "And it's time we got that trap set and ready. He's sure to come this way tonight. And we want to be ready for him."

So it was that Pete and Kennie selected the smallest lamb they could catch and placed him in the back compartment of the trap. There he would be protected by a maze of iron bars, yet would be an inviting sight for a hungry panther. Then the gate to the main compartment of the trap was raised and the trigger mechanism put in place. Next they rounded up the rest of the sheep and locked them in the barn.

Pete backed off and surveyed the works of his hands with a full measure of pride. He assured Kennie over and over again that the lamb would be perfectly safe. The trap itself, he insisted, was strong enough to keep the panther locked in once he was inside and the gate had fallen.

Pete's mind then turned to ham and baked beans, so he went to the house to visit with Nancy while she cooked. Kennie, in the meantime, would finish putting his hay away and do his chores before he came in.

It turned out to be a delightful meal. Nancy's cooking was as tasty as usual and Pete's spirits were high. He was proud of his work and Nancy continued to praise him for his great effort. After dinner Kennie loaded Pete in the car and drove him home.

Kennie in the meantime was in a state of uncertainty. He wanted Pete to succeed, yet he didn't want Old Crooked Toe in that trap. If it happened he believed he would have only one choice. He would have to do something that he did not want to do.

CHAPTER 6

K ennie and Nancy were hardly out of bed the following morning when someone banged loudly on the back door. Kennie opened the door and Pete rushed in. He muttered and sputtered but didn't get anything understandable said.

"Calm down Pete," Kennie said, "Are you trying to tell us that Old Crippled Toe has destroyed the trap?"

"No no," Pete said a little more calmly. "That old rascal, that old devil didn't come near the trap. That's the problem."

"Well," Kennie said. "Just get yourself together and tell us what happened that has you so upset."

"It's like he knew just who built that trap for him," Pete said. "It's like he was trying to get even or something of the kind."

"Then just what did he do?" Kennie asked.

"He stole my pig!" Pete blurted out. "Took it right out of the barn. I knowed better than to leave the barn door open but I forgot. So when I went to feed the pig this morning it wasn't there. The door to his stall was still closed but the top plank to the stall was missing. So was the pig!"

"Are you sure there was no way the pig could have gotten out of the stall?" Kennie asked. "Did you check the back side of the stall?"

"I checked everything," Pete said. "Fact is, I did hear something during the night. My little dog kept barking and he wouldn't come out from under the back porch. So I got my gun and flashlight and looked all around. Didn't see a living thing, but when I flashed the light around the front of the barn and I saw the door was open. So I went and shut the door without looking inside."

"We can't be sure," Kennie said, "but it does sound like Old Crooked Toe. Pete, I don't want you to worry about the pig. I have more in my pen than I am going to butcher this winter. After breakfast we'll go over and fix your stall. Then I'll see to it that there is a pig in your barn before the day is over."

After breakfast Kennie asked his mother to go with them and she accepted. So they drove over to Pete's place, and checked out the pig stall. There was no openings that the pig could have gotten through. The mystery was that they found the missing plank from the stall out back of the barn.

"Why did he carry it out here?" Pete exclaimed.

"Maybe he was trying to hide evidence," Kennie suggested.

Finally, there was something to laugh about.

Later, Kennie and Pete loaded one of Kennie's pigs in a crate and, sure enough, there was a pig in Pete's barn before the day was over.

Pete's story, coming on the heels of his building the trap, spread rapidly across the valley. It was great news to those who had insisted that Old Crooked Toe possessed some sort of mystical powers.

"I've told you he was psychic," one said. Others, tying the Beeler brothers loss to that of Pete's and adding in the recent experience on top of the cliffs, believed they had positive evidence to prove their theory.

When the latest news spread to the north end of the valley, Donnie Loudin wanted to add his bit to the boiling pot. He bad been instrumental in hiring a professional hunter some years back. As would be expected, every little bit of evidence was welcomed.

The story of Old Crooked Toe soon found its way out of the valley. Before long it became the talk of the town of Blue Sulphur Springs, which was just across the East Hills. When the editor of "The Morning Cloak" heard bits of the story he decided to send a reporter. He envisioned a piece that could be serialized in a number of issues. Bobby Cain, the young reporter, was told to check with Katie Bonner, who worked at the bank.

Katie talked briefly to the reporter when he showed up at the bank. She suggested that he talk with either Jerry Beeler or Bill Little and told him how to find each of them. She was sure Kennie would not look forward to being grilled by a reporter so she did not mention his name.

The reporter caught Jerry at a great time, out in the back yard in his favorite lounge chair, enjoying the fall sun. When he found out that Bobby was little more than a kid, just starting as a reporter, he really laid it on. He told how the old panther seemed to be defying him and his brother Tom when they brought in two trained cat hounds. He explained that Old Crooked Toe had come almost within sight of the chained dogs to kill a four-month old calf. And how he had taken time to stuff himself right there in the open.

Jerry then explained the great chase in detail. He took Bobby across the valley and up to the cliff where the old panther had eluded his pursuers.

He went into detail about Kennie Reeves harrowing experience with the old rope and emphasized the part he himself had played, both in saving Kennie and in caring for Ralph Billups when he had the heart attack.

Then he elaborated on Kennie's miraculous rescue.

"It was a miracle," he said. "That rotten rope could have broken at any point while Kennie was dangling there on the cliff face and sent him to his death forty feet down. But it didn't. Thanks be to God it didn't.

"When I realized the situation, I began to talk to God seriously. And I know He heard me. The rope held until we had a good hold on Kennie and was able to pull him to safety. It didn't just happen, it was made to happen. You can call it whatever you want. I say it was a miracle."

By the time they got out of the mountain it was well past noon. Jerry took Bobby down to Joe's Place and treated him to a sandwich and drink.

As usual, there were loafers at the station. Bobby talked to them, and also got a lengthy statement from Sam Landers, the station attendant. Then Sam told him about a young panther that had showed up some years back.

"We branded him an interloper as soon as we heard his call," Sam said. "It was a lot milder than Old Crooked Toes. His behavior was quite different, too. He screamed a lot, all during the night. It bothered the children, even some of the old folks, too."

"He didn't kill anything big, such as sheep or calves. Several cats disappeared and two small dogs came up missing — all at night. And there were suckling pigs, and chickens. He must have dearly loved chicken, because he picked them up during the day. He had the ability to get in, grab a big fat laying hen, then get away before he was discovered."

"Hunting parties went after the interloper a number of times, both in the East Hills and the mountain. Yet wherever they were, he would let out a call from the opposite side of the valley. One time he showed up right out in the center of the valley while the hunting party was up near the top of the mountain.

"We finally got rid of that big problem in a rather amusing way," Sam said. "The interloper had slipped down one of those little ravines where a spring branch joined the creek. From there, he darted into Squire McGrady's back yard, grabbed a chicken and headed for the mountain.

"But he had to go by the ball park over next to the foot of the mountain. It happened that some of the young folks were playing ball and, of course, some had brought their dogs along. Hearing the chicken squall, the dogs took up chase, keeping their distance of course. Then some of the braver boys decided to follow. It was an amusing scene until that young panther hit the mountain top, where he ran smack dab into Old Crooked Toe.

"That old panther let out a scream that would have curled your hair and sailed into the interloper like a demon. Both the dogs and the boys turned tail and ran. It's been said that the boys beat the dogs to the foot of the mountain.

"The fight lasted only a minute or two. Everyone was certain that Old Crooked Toe had put the cleaner on that interloper and sent him on his way. They also figured that the old panther had chicken for lunch that day.

"We felt certain that Old Crooked Toe had come back for the sole purpose of protecting his turf. Shortly after the fight he appeared on the cliff top and screamed. It was the first and only time he had called in the middle of the day. That night, no livestock came up missing. It was several months before that old panther returned to the valley."

Bobby Cain had been taking Sam's story on a tape recorder and all the while he had been taking notes on a pad.

"Some of the folks made mention of an old-time trapper and possibly a professional hunter having been brought in to try to take out the old panther," Bobby said. "Can you tell me anything about them?"

Sam answered, "I have heard something about them. But they were here well before I came into the valley. I expect Kennie Reeves could give you the best information about them."

Bobby said that he would be back the following day. But it was two days before the young reported returned. He had so many notes and recordings that it had taken a full day to unravel them and put them in some order for his article.

Sam talked briefly with Bobby, adding a few things that he had missed previously, then sent him to see Bill Little.

What Bill had to say ran along the same line as that of Jerry Beeler. He added a bit to an item or two that Jerry had not covered fully. Also, like Sam he believed Kennie Reeves would give him the best information about the trapper and the hired hunter.

CHAPTER 7

Kennie was cleaning out the barn when the reporter arrived that morning. Bobby Cain introduced himself and explained the purpose of his visit.

"They tell me that I will get my best information from you," Bobby said. "I hope you don't mind talking to me."

Kennie had been expecting the visit and had placed two chairs under the big shade tree in his back yard.

"Let's go sit under the tree down there," he said. "I may be able to help you some. I was talking to Bill Little last night and he told me to expect you."

"What prompted you to become a reporter?" Kennie asked when they were seated. "You look like you should be in college."

"I was in college briefly," Bobby said. "I majored in journalism, but I dropped out."

"Didn't you like it?" Kennie asked.

"I only had one semester behind me when my father died," Bobby said.

"I'm sorry to hear that," Kenny said. "But is that a reason to quit college?"

"Mom was sick and I couldn't afford to hire someone to care for her," Bobby said. "And with Dad gone, I couldn't afford to stay in college anyway. Luckily for me, the editor of the local paper made a place for me. But I'm the one who is supposed to be asking all the questions.""

"Okay," Kennie smiled, then he turned and gazed across the valley. "What is it that you want from me?"

"Well, some of the locals I talked to think you don't want to kill that old panther," Bobby said. "Maybe I shouldn't ask …"

"You can ask me anything you want," Kennie said. "But, my answer to that question is that everyone has a right to their own opinion."

The young reporter hesitated for several seconds, then proceeded.

"One thing we keep hearing from people in the valley, something that helped create an interest in this story, is that the old panther is psychic," he said, and then he paused.

"How do you feel about the psychic bit?" Bobby resumed. "Do you think Old Crooked Toe is psychic?"

"I guess it is up to one's interpretation of the word psychic," Kennie said. "As for me, I would hesitate to describe Old Crooked Toe as psychic."

"What about when the Beeler brothers brought in those trained cat hounds?" Bobby continued. "Also, the panther's actions when that man named Pete built a trap for him?"

"All I know is that God has built into some animals mental powers which we mortals do not understand," Kennie replied.

"What about the professional hunter and the professional trapper who both had what both Sam Landers and Bill Little said were, and I quote, 'mystical experiences' ?"

"Well," said Kennie, "As to the professional trapper, we didn't bring him in. A man claiming to have been a professional trapper for a number of years in Alaska just showed up one day.

"He was a strange looker — heavy beard, long hair. The car he was driving looked like it had been rescued from a junk yard. Still, he told some great tales about his trapping experiences. Most folks believed him at first. Then the stories started to get a bit hairy and his role as a hero grew with each telling.

"There was an old log cabin over in the maple trees at the foot of the mountain. It had, at one time, been used during sugaring season for shelter while boiling the sugar water down into syrup. He moved into that cabin, did a bit of fixing up, and made it his headquarters. It wasn't much, but I guess that it served the purpose for someone who had been used to make-do in the wilds of Alaska."

"Someone told me his name was Banjo Hobo," Bobby said. "Is that true?"

Kenny shook his head in amusement. "Banjo Hobo? Yes, and claimed he had heard about a panther that couldn't be put down. Said he was going to 'take the critter out' - his words. That's how he described it. Spent a lot of time in the mountain and back in the Monongahela. After some weeks he claimed he had unraveled the panther's pattern of travel and said Old Crooked Toe would pass on a certain trail intersection above his cabin at a certain time."

Kenny laughed. "He said, and I am quoting him - 'I'm going to pinch his toes tomorrow night at twelve midnight.' And he showed us a large trap and said it was a bear trap."

Bobby asked about the trap.

"Several valley residents objected to that big trap being set so close to the valley. They said it was a hazard to the local children and dogs who roamed freely in the mountain. But he paid no attention to them, and he set the trap anyway.

"The next day was sunny, but mild, with a gentle breeze out of the northwest. Everything seemed perfect, that is, until midnight when Old Crooked Toe was supposed to pass through. There was a full moon, then the sky just went pitch black. There were volleys of thunder, and lightning streaked across the sky. Then the wind picked up, and it began to hail.

"We lost our power. The hail stones at my house were about pea size, maybe a little bigger. Over at the foot of the mountain, according to Banjo, they were more like baseballs.

"When some of us went to look, we were not inclined to disagree with his statement. The windshield of his old car was destroyed. All of the glass in the doors was broken. The roof of his cabin had been pulverized. He had brought in his trap by the time we got there. He said that the hail stones had triggered it and damaged the pan.

"Banjo had Bub Little, Bill Little's son, drive him to town. He bought another old car at Fraley's Auto Barn. Paid cash. Then, that night he just disappeared. No one knew where he came from. No one knew where he went.

"Bub said that night he drove Banjo in, he blamed Old Crooked Toe for all his problems. He said he wanted to get completely away from that panther and no amount of money could get him back in the Monongahela.

"The old car he left behind sat at the cabin for two years before the owner of the cabin had Floyd Jenkins come and haul it off. Floyd later said that their wasn't any registration in the glove box, and the serial number had been filed off of the engine block."

Bobby took time to change tapes on his recorder.

"Now," he asked Kennie, "what do you know about the hired hunter?

"Not a lot," Kennie said. "I do know that some of the farmers up in the north end of the valley contributed to a fund to bring in a professional hunter. They did that after Old Crooked Toe made his one and only kill up that way. Cory Long's brother Lemuel was one of those raising the money. Cory said they finally found someone who was willing to go after the panther. Whether he was really a professional hunter, I don't know. Cory said that he hunted a couple days, spent the second night in the Monongahela, and then he was back by noon of the third day. Has anyone already told you this?"

Bobby shook his head no and Kennie continued.

"He had a weird story about coming face to face with the panther. Cory said the man claimed he had a bead on the panther. He pulled the trigger and the gun went off, but there was no panther. He said it scared him something fierce. Then, when he whirled the other way to run, the panther was smack dab in the middle of the trail again, right there in front of him. By then he was so frightened he just took out through the brush. He said he didn't know whether the panther was following him or not. He didn't look back until he was out of the Monongahela. Cory said the man refused to go back in the big forest again.

"If you want more on that I'm sure Lemuel will be willing to help you As for us here in the south end of the valley, we could only take in what we heard, even if it did sound a little bizarre."

Bobby stopped the recorder. He looked directly into Kennie's eyes. "You've given me a lot of good information, which I really appreciate. But what about that great story everyone tells me you have?"

Kennie looked long at Bobby and smiled.

"You're not the first one who has hit me with that question," he said. "It's true, I do have a story to tell. When the time is right I'll tell it."

"I'm sure it would help with my reporting career," Bobby said.

"I'll make you a bargain," Kennie said. "If you'll do what I ask you to do, I'll let you in on the initial telling of my story. When I give you the time and the place you're to tell no one. When you come, come alone. There'll be no story if there's a crowd."

"I wouldn't have it any other way," Bobby promised. "It will be my exclusive."

Kennie nodded.

"Before you leave, go by the bank and give Katie Bonner both your personal and business phone numbers. When it happens, she'll call you with the time and place."

Bobby stood and said, "This is exciting! I'll handle it just the way you want."

Kennie stood and shook Bobby's hand. "I have another suggestion for you if you're interested. Talk to Pete Higgins, the man who made the trap you mentioned. Pete is a great guy. If he is willing to tell you his personal story it would make a great human interest article. However, I will ask that you get Pete's permission before you do an article on him, the personal story that is, not the story about the trap. He is very sensitive. He does not like to be called a hero. He says he was only doing what Jesus would want him to do. I'll give you a brief bit of why you will find Pete so crippled.

"It happened something like four, maybe five years ago, in the town where you live and work. Pete had gone there shopping with his wife Molly. They were visiting with friends -- Pete has lots of friends -- when he saw a car speeding down the street. He also saw a toddler who had gotten away from her mother and wandered out into the path of the oncoming car.

"Without hesitation Pete leaped out into the street and grabbed the child. He whirled and attempted to leap out of the path of the oncoming car. The driver never slowed, never swerved.

"Pete almost made it. Almost but not quite. The car struck him full and sent him flying. He rolled over a couple times. When they got to Pete he was unconscious, but his arms were still locked tight about little Becky Lee, the child he was attempting to save. When they loosened his arms they found she didn't have a scratch. But Pete was a mess.

"Just four months before Becky had lost her father to a drunken driver. Her mother, Pamela Lee, was still trying to get over the loss of her husband. You can imagine how grateful she was to Pete for saving her daughter --her only child."

Kennie listed Pete's injuries which included both legs broken, one with a compound fracture; severe trauma to his back; and scrapes, cuts and bruises head to toe.

"Pete's recovery was months long and painful. Shortly after he got back on his feet, his wife Molly died. They had no children, but if you think Pete was left alone you are wrong.

"Pamela has a big happy family and none have forgotten what Pete did for Becky. On holidays, including Christmas and Thanksgiving, Pete is included in the family celebration. They consider him a part of their family.

"On pretty days when Pam isn't working, they some times bring a picnic basket and take Pete over to the foot of the mountain and have lunch under some of those lovely sugar maple trees. Becky has adopted Pete as a Grandpa. When she comes, she brings her friends and they all call him Grandpa Pete. He loves it."

Kennie asked: "Do you know Susan Lee at the bank?"

Bobby said he did.

"Well, she's a relative and I am certain she would give you an interview. In the meantime, I will shut up and let you get going. You need to talk to Pete."

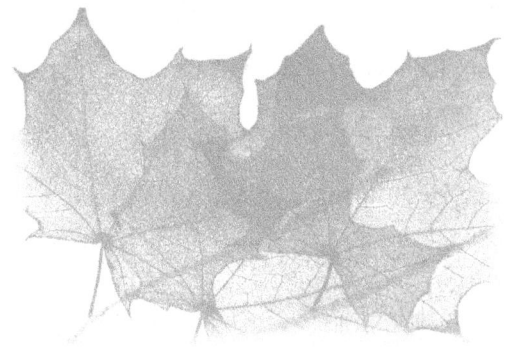

CHAPTER 8

It was some time before Old Crooked Toe came back to Cave Creek valley. Yet it seemed there was always something exciting or frightening going on in that little secluded community. This time it was a pack of wild dogs that harassed the residents. They were not real wild dogs, just domestic dogs that had formed a pack and were living off of the land; and the farms. As they became more aggressive they threatened the children to the point that many of the residents took measures to protect their little ones.

Cory Long was one of those who built a play pen outside the house. Since he worked away so much he wanted a secure place where Agnes could get the children outside safely. He had two children, one seven the other five. He made the pen large enough that the neighbors two children could join his own when they chose.

Others in the community took their children to the school playground where they were protected by armed adults.

THE MIRACLES OF SUGAR MAPLE MOUNTAIN

In a matter of only a few weeks the dog pack had killed or maimed several times more sheep than Old Crooked Toe had killed in a seven-year span. This slaughter caught the attention of all farmers whether they raised sheep or not. So they began to organize hunting parties.

The dog pack spent most of their time in the East Hills. That was rougher terrain, lots of thick brush, and of course better hiding places. Then they did their raiding at night. But as more and more farmers took measures to protect their animals at night the pack became more hungry and more aggressive. Kennie joined a hunting party twice and on each occasion spent a full day wandering about in the woods without any sign of the pack.

Jerry Beeler discovered that the pack was using the same deep draw that Old Crooked Toe had used to enter and slip out of the East Hills. So some of the farmers began to take turns hiding in the entrance to the draw and finally were able to kill two of the dogs. This caused the four remaining members of the pack to become more elusive. Still they were, on many occasions, coming into the valley in full daylight.

Dudley Newberry was working in his hay one day when he heard children screaming and dogs barking. He ran around his barn to find three children backed into a corner beside the barn and a fence. The oldest boy was trying to fend off the dogs with a board. When Dudley approached the pack they charged him. He gouged the nearest one with his pitch fork and all four turned and fled.

So fear in the valley continued to grow.

It so happened about that time that Old Crooked Toe decided to make one of his quiet visits to the valley, and to the East Hills beyond. He came out of the shadowy depths of the Monongahela at midnight, using one of the game trails that would bring him to the crest of Sugar Maple Mountain about midway of the valley.

At the top of the mountain he paused and surveyed the lay of the land ahead of him. It was not an act of fear, rather of caution; the thing that had kept him alive and safe for many years. He came like a silent shadow down the face of the mountain, crossed the valley and buried himself in the wilds of the East Hills.

He was tired by a long trek from deep in the wilderness so he bedded down in a thicket until daybreak.

The old panther had hunted the East Hills for many years. He was familiar with the favorite licks and waterholes frequented by deer and other wild creatures. He selected the nearest waterhole and began to approach with much caution.

When he came in sight of the waterhole he saw a doe drinking. The distance to the waterhole was too great for a charge. Without question the deer would either hear him, or maybe just look around and see him. He paused. To the right stood a heavy clump of undergrowth that would be within charging distance.

He dropped back and, moving as quietly as possible, came in behind the clump. The doe had her head up. He waited until she dropped her head again to drink. That was when he moved.

He came in swiftly, two great bounds and he was on top of the deer, catching her just as she attempted to spring away. He drove her to the ground, dispatched her swiftly, then drug the still quivering body away to the nearest secluded nook. In the quiet cool of the deep forest he feasted, stuffed his hungry middle to contentment. Then it was time for another nap.

He found a dense thicket and slept.

Old Crooked Toe awoke with a start. He heard growling, chewing sounds. He stood up, peeped out of his thicket where he had found cover and saw four dogs gnawing at his kill. He lunged out of the thicket and charged the dogs with flailing forearms.

The dogs retreated but did not flee. They were hungry. In fact they were famished and they were willing to fight for food. They raged, darting in and out, staying always beyond those flailing forepaws that were armed with knife-like claws. It was apparent that the dogs were trying to wear the panther down by having him charge first one then the other. But the panther had fought too many battles for that to work. He backed up to his kill, lashing out only when a dog got close in.

The fight lasted for several minutes and ended only when Old Crooked Toe was finally able to make contact. He ripped the side of one of his attackers with a light blow. The dog gave a yelp and fled. The other three backed off and they too raced away when the panther charged.

Old Crooked Toe went back, lay down beside his kill and dozed again. What had brought the old panther back to the valley and the East Hills was a shortage of game in the Monongahela. Parts of the forest had been opened up to deer hunters and they had flocked to the forest. They killed many deer, wounded more and drove those remaining into hiding. Now with a stuffed middle, the old panther was ready to return to his haunts deep in his forest, that great wild land known as the Monongahela.

About mid afternoon Old Crooked Toe nibbled again at the scant remaining meat on his kill and turned back West. He was comfortably full so he had no need to hurry. He walked slowly, deliberately, following the back of a long ridge that led to the foot of the hills. The valley was narrow here so he decided to dash to the creek, wade it, then lope across to Sugar Maple Mountain before he could be apprehended.

As the panther approached the edge of the wooded land he heard dogs barking. He paused, listened. He had survived many chases in his time, so barking dogs always got his immediate attention. Then he recognized the baying of the dogs as that of the four that had feasted on his kill and had fought him earlier in the day.

He paused for a moment, hesitating. He had wanted to exit the hills quietly. Yet the urge to be at those intruders was compelling.

He took a step forward, then paused. There were other sounds, screams of children and a woman. Yet the urge to get at those intruders who had dared stand up to him was too great. He lunged down the hill.

When he came into the open he saw the dogs. Saw them tearing at a gate on a pen. Saw them trying to get at the children in the pen. Then not far away was a woman screaming.

It was a scene that the old panther would normally have fled from. Yet there before him were the four dogs that had gnawed on his kill and had fought him viciously. Without hesitation he lunged from his vantage position on the bank above the yard.

He landed on top of the pack before they saw him. His great forearms were flailing even before he landed. His jaws were widespread. He broke the back of one dog with a blow from a heavy left forepaw, another with the right forearm. He caught the head of another in his opened jaws. That dog died instantly. The fourth dog saw what was happening and was able to leap away and dash to the safety of nearby brush.

CHAPTER 9

A gnes Long stood horrified. Things were happening too fast. One tragic moment had passed. A moment when her greatest fear was that the dogs would get through the gate and tear her children to pieces. And when it seemed that the dogs were close to doing just that, she had gone to God for help.

Agnes had stopped screaming long enough to pray. She had closed her eyes and, in the strongest voice she could muster, she begged God to save her children. When she opened her eyes there was the panther, landing right on top of the dog pack. In one fleeting moment she had seen the panther's outstretched left forearm break the back of one dog, his right forearm do the same to the dog on the other side. And right beneath his body was the third dog, crushed down by his weight and unable to move.

Yes, one tragic moment had passed, but was she now faced with another. Would the panther now tear her children apart, just as she had feared the dogs would do?

Agnes wanted to dash inside the house and find Cory's rifle, but she found herself unable to move. She had stopped screaming. The children had stopped screaming. The dogs were no longer barking.

In what seemed an eerie silence Agnes watched the panther kill the dogs with the broken backs, saw him crush their heads in his powerful jaws then fling the lifeless bodies aside. Then he did the same thing to the dog beneath him. She saw him raise his head. He looked at her. He looked at the children. She thought her heart was going to beat its way right out of her breast.

It was when Old Crooked Toe looked at Agnes again that she felt a wave of relief pass over her. His ears were not flat on his head, nor his lips curled as they had been when he was killing the dogs. And as their eyes met and held for seconds, she felt that she was seeing something close to friendship.

Then, to her amazement, Agnes watched the old panther turn slowly and walk away. His head was high. He exhibited no need to hurry. He walked down to the creek. He never looked back He exhibited the elation of a king that had just won a major battle.

Agnes saw him wade the creek, saw him at last hit that long rolling lope that carried him swiftly across the valley to the foot of the mountain. Only then, when the woods seemed to open up and swallow him, was she able to take her eyes away from the panther and back to the children

Still trembling violently, Agnes dashed to the pen, unlocked the gate and hurried the children into the house. She sat down, tried to calm herself, then called Cory at work. She attempted to tell him what had happened, but she was still shaking so violently that her words were not coherent. She hung up the phone, waited more minutes then was able to tell Cory what had happened.

"Hang on," came the reply. "I'll come now."

"Don't hurry home," Agnes hastened. "Everything is alright here. It was all like a miracle, Cory.

"It had all happened when I was inside and heard the children screaming and dogs barking. I rushed outside and there was the pack, tearing at the gate. The only thing I could see to use as a weapon was a broom I had left outside when I swept the porch. I grabbed the broom and made at the dogs. The largest dog grabbed the broom and jerked it away from me, almost pulling me into the pack. He started tearing at the gate again."

Agnes paused for a second and then continued: "I was sure he would be at the children in seconds. The only thing I knew to do was pray. And then, there he was. Old Crooked Toe came out of nowhere. He just appeared. And, he was right on top of the dogs. And he did everything so fast. In what seemed like a flash one of the dogs was dead and two of them were laying there with their backs broken.

"The only dog left was the smallest one. He was running away as fast as he could. I thought the panther was going to chase it - I hoped he would - but he didn't. He turned back to the two wounded dogs and killed them. He crushed their heads.

"When the children saw the panther they had stopped screaming. I stopped screaming. It was like we had been waiting for, even expecting him. When he landed on the dogs they stopped barking. It was a miracle Cory, I'm telling you. It had to be a miracle.

"When the panther finished with the dogs he looked at the children, he looked at me. I was frightened all over again. But he didn't growl, didn't make any kind of sound. His ears were erect, his lips were not curled. And when he looked at me the second time our eyes held for several seconds. And you may wonder about me Cory, but I actually felt something like a feeling of friendship between us."

"Don't get too worked up," Cory said. "He's still a wild animal, still dangerous."

"I'm not getting worked up," Agnes said. "I know he is still a wild animal. But I was there. I know what he did. I know how I felt when he looked at me. And we both know that God gave some animals a special sense that we humans don't understand.

"Remember the little beagle that your brother Lemuel had. She could let them know when Pansy was going to have a seizure. Lemuel could not do that, neither could Pansy's mother, Claudia."

""I know, honey," Cory said. "I wasn't meaning to be critical. Tell me what happened then."

"He just turned away and started walking toward the creek. To me he looked like a king. He walked like a king. It was as though he was proud of what he had done. And you know something Cory, I couldn't take my eyes off of Old Crooked Toe until he had crossed the creek, loped across the valley and the woodlands just seemed to open up and swallow him.

"That was when I finally was able to move, to get to the children and get us all in the house.

"Don't you ever again help anyone who tries to kill that panther. Please promise me, Cory, that you will never do anything to hurt that old panther. He saved our children, Cory. I saw him do it. He saved our children."

"Don't you worry," Cory said. "Just you and the kids get yourselves calmed down and we'll have a long talk when I get home. Before we go to bed tonight we'll thank God for a good ending to what must certainly have looked to you like a very bad situation. And we'll thank Him, not just with our lips, but with our minds and hearts."

CHAPTER 10

Kennie had just come in the house from doing his chores when Cory Long called. He talked for just a moment before putting Agnes on the phone to give Kennie a full account of what had happened, and Agnes didn't mince words.

After Agnes finished, Kennie hung up and just stood in a daze for several minutes before going to the table to sit. Nancy listened in silence while he told her the full story, just as Agnes had related it to him.

When Kennie finished Nancy sat watching her son, and remembering. She was seeing the younger man, now more than six years ago. Hearing once again the promise. Those words just seemed to keep coming back to haunt Nancy. So, once again she encouraged Kennie to make a life for himself, a life with Katie. Yet again she received the same response.

"I'm happy running the farm the way Dad wanted me to run it when he was alive," Kennie said. "And Katie is happy with her work at the bank. Her

Dad really needs her more than you need me."

When the conversation ended, Nancy sat watching her son stare. She knew he was not looking at the wall or even the window. His mind was seeing something from that mysterious past.

Abruptly Kennie turned to his mother and said, "This is great news, not only to Cory and Agnes, but also to those who care about the old panther. And maybe that last statement applies to me. I know you have to be aware of the fact that I have a special feeling for Old Crooked Toe.

"I think I'll call Katie," he continued. "I'll have her get this story to Bobby Cain when she goes to the bank tomorrow."

"You're too late," Katie said when Kennie started to tell her what had happened. "Agnes already called me. She told me the full story and wanted me to tell Bobby what happened. She would like to talk to him herself. So the first thing I will do when I get to work tomorrow will be to talk to Bobby.

"Incidentally, Bobby did a fabulous job on his other story. The town people simply ate it up.

"The editor broke his article into a series and is still publishing parts of it. I'm saving all of the bank's copies. I'll bring you the full series," she laughed. "And, I might add, Bobby has made you quite a hero, or something of the sort."

"I'm no hero," Kennie said. "I did try to help him because of the things that have happened to him. I'll do anything I can for him. He can write a good article about Agnes now. She really lays it on the line."

A few days later Kennie saw Pete and told him in great detail what had happened.

Pete just shook his head.

"He's still a dangerous wild animal," he said. "He just happened to be at the right place at the right time. He stole my pig and I haven't forgiven him."

When Bobby got the word, he came at once to interview Agnes. She was ready for him.

"Cory and I didn't actually think that there was a need for a pen for the children," Agnes said. "Yet when others began to take steps to protect their children we decided maybe we should do something. Thank God Cory did build that enclosure. He thought he had a sufficiently strong gate, but when he checked it after the attack he said another minute or two and the dogs would have been in on the children.

"I don't know where that panther came from. I had my eyes glued on the dogs. Then I did the only thing I could think of, I closed my eyes and prayed. And let me tell you Bobby Cain, I prayed as hard as I knew how. When I opened my eyes he was right on top of the dogs. I told Cory and I'm telling you Bobby, it was a miracle. The way Old Crooked Toe came, it was a miracle."

Agnes went on to tell Bobby about the two lambs the dogs had taken from Jeb Hubble's flock of sheep. And there were other animals and chickens that had fallen prey to the dog pack. She told him to talk to Dudley Newberry about how he saved the children from the pack.

When they finished the interview, Agnes gave Bobby sufficient money to buy a dozen copies of the issue that carried his article about her experience. He was to send them by either Susan Lee or Katie Bonner and have them left with Sam Landers at the service station to be handed out to ones who wanted them.

Once again Old Crooked Toe had gained some points in his favor. Yet, like the time he ran off the intruder, he soon blew his points.

CHAPTER 11

It was about two months later that the old panther announced his presence from atop the cliffs on Sugar Maple Mountain. Yet no animals disappeared for two nights. Some of the folks guessed he was hunting the East Hills, but he was not. He was laying out in the mountain above the north end of the valley. And then he struck.

Lemuel Long, Cory's brother, went out the next morning to discover a two-month old calf missing. There was a trail of blood over the fence at the end of the calf lot. It led off toward the mountain until it faded away.

Cory had talked to Lemuel about Agnes' experience, but the folks up on the north end of the valley were not very tolerant. They valued their private way of life. That privacy had been invaded again. So, before the day was half spent there was a sizable hunting party organized.

Their plan was for five men to climb to the top of the mountain. They were then to spread out with a short distance between them. Then the six others were to spread out up the mountainside and all start walking south. They hoped that the panther had feasted somewhere along the face of the mountain and that the drivers would send him up to those above.

When everyone had time to get in place Lemuel sounded the start with his hunting horn. So the hunt began. They traveled all the way to the south end of the mountain, but no panther. The ones on the face of the mountain took new positions and they began traveling north.

Somewhere, nearing the mountain side above Lemuel's farm, one of the hunters found the place where Old Crooked Toe had feasted. There were the scant remains of his kill. Nearby they found where he had been sleeping in a thicket. The coy old panther had been aware of what was going on. He had simply lain quietly until all hunters had passed. Then he slipped to the top of the mountain, dropped off on the other side and was, by now, well on his way to his secret coves somewhere in the vastness of that sprawling National Forest.

Knowing what had happened after Agnes' experience, Lemuel sent word to Bobby Cain to come and get another story about the old panther. He wanted the other side of Old Crooked Toe to be revealed.

When first Old Crooked Toe had announced his presence on this last visit, Pete Higgins had hobbled over to Kennie's place. He had insisted that now was the time to once again bait and set the trap and that was what they had done. Then for the next two mornings he had visited the trap at the crack of dawn. And two times was disappointed.

Then had come word of what had happened up on the north end of the valley. So the lamb was released from the bait end of the trap and Pete went wearily home. No panther this time, yet Pete hadn't given up. He was certain there would be another time.

Old Crooked Toe did not put in his appearance for a long spell. Residents of the valley began to speculate about what could have happened. Life in the valley might have become rather humdrum if it had not been for Bobby Cain's frequent visits. The old panther had got him off to a good start with his reporting and he didn't miss an opportunity to show up.

He wrote articles about the Beeler brothers and how they had both got started in the medical field while serving their country in the military, Jerry in the army and Tom in the navy. And though Bobby carried his camera, he was delighted when both brothers had photos of themselves from their military days in service uniforms.

Then there was Lemuel Long who had retired from the Army as a Lieutenant Colonel after a long period of service. When the editor of the newspaper wanted more news about Lemuel, Bobby came back. It seemed the editor was also a retired army officer. In each case Bobby learned more about how to flush information out of his subject, and he was loving it.

At every opportunity, Bobby found somewhere to get in a mention of Kennie Reeves. When he found that Kennie's mother had been a school teacher at one time he jumped at the opportunity to do an article on her. It made interesting reading for others in the valley, but it also gave Bobby an excuse for mentioning Kennie.

When Bobby found that the residents of the valley were exceptionally proud of their massive sugar maple trees he set about finding someone who had engaged in sugaring, as they called it. He wanted someone who had worked it as a business in the past. That man turned out to be Dudley Newberry, who just happened to be the oldest resident of the valley.

Dudley was thrilled at the opportunity to talk about the business that he had loved and worked for many seasons. He went into the house over the cellar and dug out the tools of the trade -- a brace and bit, a couple home-made wooden spiels and a bucket. Armed with these, they walked over to the foot of the Mountain.

With Bobby busy with his camera, Dudley demonstrated how the trees were tapped and the sweet water caught in buckets. Then they went into the log shed where the water was boiled down to make highly flavored syrup. The furnace, made of field sandstones was in a state of disrepair, but it was still visible. Hanging on the back wall of the shed was the home made pan used in the boiling process.

Dudley went into detail explaining how the leaves of the tree gathered the dextrose from sunlight, stored it in the roots of the tree, then how the changing of seasons brought the sweet water back up through the veins of the tree trunk.

"Then came the process of boiling, checking for thickness and the tasting,"

Dudley said.

So Bobby went away with another article that would be read with interest by all, especially residents of the valley. Indeed, by now Bobby bad created so much interest in his newspaper that most of the residents of the valley were subscribers to The Morning Cloak. Of course that pleased Kenneth King, the editor.

Bobby Cain had become a regular at the service station. He had long ago discovered that was the focal point of the community. Sometimes he needed to ask questions. Sometimes he just listened.

Now he was listening to lots of speculation about why Old Crooked Toe had been absent so long. So he determined to do an article just asking residents two questions. The first question would be -- "What do you think has happened to the old panther?" The second -- "Do you hope he returns to the valley?" So that was what he set about, and he talked with a number of the residents.

To what they thought might have happened to Old Crooked Toe, he got a wide variety of possibilities. They ranged from someone, somewhere killing him, to he just plain did not want to return. Then to Bobby's surprise he found that more hoped that the old panther would return, than those who hoped he would never come back to the valley again.

Residents of the valley who had taken part in the survey awaited anxiously for the results. Then one day the paper with the survey arrived late in the afternoon.

So, while many were reading the results that evening, they heard a familiar sound. From far up atop the rugged sandstone cliffs of Sugar Maple Mountain, it came -- Old Crooked Toe's announcement of his return. This time his scream seemed a little more piercing, a little louder, and for the first time he screamed twice, one long call and a shorter, milder scream.

CHAPTER 12

As Kennie expected, it wasn't long until Pete showed up. He wasn't as jubilant as Kennie had expected him to be. Yet once again they got the trap in readiness.

"This is the time," Pete insisted. "He hasn't paid you a call for some time, so expect him tonight and you are going to see that my trap works. Maybe some of my previous ideas were a bit screwball, but not the trap. I've put a lot of work and thought in that thing. I just simply have the feeling that this will be the night."

Somehow, yet he did not know why, Kennie had the same feeling. It was somewhat like an apprehension of doom. The night might bring on another failure, yet it could bring on a decision that he had hoped never to have to make. Pete wanted to talk about the trap, the panther, but Kennie had no desire to discuss either. So he hustled Pete off to the house and suggested that he and Nancy visit while she prepared dinner and he did his evening chores.

Kennie needed to get his mind on something away from his fears. So he got his scythe and assailed the weed patch back of the barn. He did his chores and found other odd jobs to keep him busy until Pete came out and told him his mother wanted him to come in and get ready for dinner.

Pete and Nancy soon recognized Kennie's mood, so they found other topics to talk about. A snake had gotten into the school house up in the northern end of the valley and frightened some of the students. Yet some of the older boys had really enjoyed chasing the snake all over the room before they got it out of the house.

Then Pete told about the last weekend when Pam and Becky Lee had brought out a car load of Becky's friends. They had also brought a full picnic basket and spent another pleasurable evening at the foot of the mountain beneath the sugar maple trees.

After dinner Kennie drove Pete home and, strangely enough, neither mentioned the trap or the panther. Pete found it convenient to discuss further the last visit from Pam and Becky Lee, and Kennie was willing to just listen.

Kennie went to his room early, but he did not go to bed for some time. He sat for a long while on the side of the bed, deep in thought. He was convincing himself that there were times in life when one must do that which he does not want to do. With that fixed in his mind he went to bed and went to sleep. Yet that fact did not allay the bad dreams that plagued him throughout the night. He would wake up and try to get his mind on something else. Yet that dream would come back, and, each time there was always the panther looking at him as he had looked on that fateful night almost eight years ago.

Kennie was up early, but he did not go at once to do his chores. Instead he watched Nancy prepare breakfast and waited for a knock on the door. It wasn't long before that knock came.

As expected, it was Pete, but his expression showed no elation. So Kennie knew before Pete spoke that nothing had happened.

"Come in Pete and have a seat while Mom finishes breakfast," Kennie said.

"Dasted cat," Pete said. "I was sure that pig stealing rascal would be there waiting for me this morning. Guess he had other ideas."

Pete was right. Old Crooked Toe did have other ideas. Under cover of darkness he had crossed the valley and buried himself deep in the East Hills.

Some years back he had hunted the farms on beyond the hills. It had been only a couple times, but each hunt had been successful. He had, on each occasion, left the area and hurried back to the sanctity of the Monongahela, his middle stuffed with sweet red meat.

On that first night the panther did not strike. Instead he cruised the edge of the forest, checking the lay of the land, selecting the farm he would strike, and strike he did.

He waited until well after midnight. It was something he had long ago learned. That was the time when most folks would be sound asleep. It was also the time that most animals would be bedded down. Then there were the dogs. They would probably be sound asleep on the back porch, or maybe under it.

So that was when he would make his move.

He came out of the shadows and padded quietly along the side of a plank fence until he could see a cow and her calf bedded down on the inside of the lot. They were near the fence. Still slinking low to the ground, he backed a bit from the fence, then leaped.

He landed almost on top of the calf. In what seemed like a singular motion, he smashed the animal back to the ground with his right paw as it tried to get up. With lightning-like speed he tore out it's throat before it could issue a sound.

Old Crooked Toe had made a kill. One that he was pleased with. He stood there with a paw on the animal until it was dead. He then grasped it by a leg and drug it to the fence. Only then did he realize that the animal was too big to be carried over the fence, and he was dangerously close to a building. It was a situation he didn't like. Yet he had heard no sound of running feet, no dog-like sounds. Still he looked, listened. Then he feasted.

When he had fed to contentment there was a greater part of a hind quarter missing, The belly had been torn open and the heart and liver had been consumed. Then, slowly, deliberately, he leaped over the fence and wandered back into the wilderness.

The old panther saw no need to hurry. On each of the two previous visits he had paid the Blue Lick area there had been no dogs sent on his trail. Instead there had been hunting parties, but he had found it easy to elude those noisy hunters both times. So he was slightly more than a half mile into the forest when he decided to bed down, and he didn't move until he heard the baying of hounds.

CHAPTER 13

When Barry Sanchez went out to do his milking the morning following Old Crooked Toe's visit, he was surprised to find the cows all gathered in the far end of the barn lot. He was driving them back toward the barn when he realized his prize heifer calf was not with her mother. He was close to the barn before he saw the calf laying near the fence. He hurried the cows inside, got them into their stalls, then went to check the calf.

Barry had bred one of his Holstein cows to a Jersey bull in hopes of improving the quality of his milk. He had a small dairy operation and sold milk only to local families.

At first Barry decided that the wildcats had struck again. He and his neighbors had, for years now, been plagued by a family of Bobcats that denned up in the rocky heights of Blue Lick Knob. It had been only two days since they had killed one of the cats that had been striking down lambs and small pigs.

Yet again, this was different.

When Barry considered the size of the calf, he realized that the marauder had to be much larger than the wildcat they had killed just two days ago. Then there was the way the throat had been torn out and the quantity of meat that had been consumed.

Barry did his milking and put the milk away in the cooler. When he went in to breakfast, he and his wife Kalia discussed what had happened. They talked about the two previous occasions when residents of the community had been plagued by a big cat.

Lately newspapers from a neighboring town had found their way into some of the households in their community. There had been articles about the panther that called regularly on Cave Spring Valley. So before breakfast was over they had decided who their visitor was, even to his name.

"They call him Old Crooked Toe," Kalia said.

Barry called Kandy Boder and Juan Wilmer and asked that they come right over. They were the two neighbors who had gone in with Barry to rent the four hounds that had treed the wildcat they killed just two days ago. Fortunately, they had not returned the rented hounds.

When the three men went out to take a look at the dead heifer, it didn't take them long to decide what to do. So, while the morning was still new, four experienced cat hounds were bellowing on Old Crooked Toe's trail.

"Let's listen a bit," Barry said. "We'll try to get some direction out of their baying, then we'll decide what to do."

It wasn't long until they could see that the hounds were going straight West.

"I think they are heading for Cave Creek Valley," Kandy said. "What do you think, Barry?"

"I believe we had best get out of here and around to the valley," Barry agreed. "Let's grab our guns. If we could get there ahead of the dogs we will have a better idea on what we should do. From what we have been reading about him, I feel sure that old panther is heading strait for the Monongahela."

Agnes Long was hanging clothes on the line out back when she heard the hounds singing their trail song. She sat the basket of clothes down and hurried around the house to where the children were playing with a new puppy. After the episode with the wild dogs she was still weary of barking dogs, particularly if there was more than one. What she was hearing now sounded like a pack.

She called the children to her and they got ready to hurry into the house in case they needed to. But it wasn't the dogs they saw in just a few minutes. It was Old Crooked Toe. He came down the same path he had been on the day he fought the wild dogs. He was running hard. He passed them and raced on down to the creek in great bounds. He hit the creek but did not cross it. Instead, he turned down the creek. He kept in the water, but close enough to the edge that he could keep running.

Agnes knew what the old panther was doing. He was hard pressed by the hounds and he was hiding his trail in the water. Sure enough, it was only minutes until the pack came rushing down the hill, all four of them. They hit the creek and splashed across it. They were almost a hundred feet beyond the creek when they realized they had lost the scent.

Agnes grabbed each of the kids by a hand and they hurried up the hill to where they could get a better look at the valley. By now the hounds were cruising up and down the creek bank in search of the lost trail. Then they crossed back over and checked the near bank, two going up the creek and two down. It was apparent that they were becoming more and more frantic with each sashay that found no scent.

Agnes and the kids could see the panther far across the valley, still running hard. Just as he reached the foot of the mountain one of the hounds crossed back across the creek and cut his trail. He let out a bellow that brought his pack mates splashing back across the creek to join him. Within seconds the entire pack was singing as they raced across the valley.

Then, Agnes saw a car racing down the road on the other side of the creek. It came to a stop at the service station. Three men jumped out and approached Sam Landers. She could see Sam pointing, but of course she could only guess at what he was saying. Then she saw the men go back to the car, and each came out with a rifle. She gripped the hands of the children and Arick, the tallest, heard her soft whisper: "Please, God, don't let them kill Old Crooked Toe.

Old Crooked Toe was by now deep in the mountain, the hounds were well across the valley and the three men with the rifles were hurrying in the wake of the hounds.

Agnes squeezed the hands of the kids, breathed a soft prayer into the air and turned down to the house. She hurriedly finished hanging out the clothes and went into the house, but she could not concentrate on anything.

God would take care of Old Crooked Toe. She was sure of that. Yet somehow she had to know what was taking place. Agnes and the children climbed up the hill again for another look see. By now the baying of the hounds had dimmed as they moved down the back side of Sugar Maple Mountain. The three hunters had to be well up the side of the mountain. So Agnes and the kids returned to the house.

Twice again the three climbed the hill. It was on the second trip that they were aware that the baying of the hounds had become a bit louder. Then they could tell that the chase had turned south. Maybe Old Crooked Toe was making a run for the cliffs on the south point of the mountain. Agnes hoped so, but those hopes were soon dashed. She heard the pack's baying change. They were now singing the treed song. Then several minutes, maybe a half an hour and she heard shots, two of them. She gripped the hands of the kids and turned down the hill, sobbing softly.

Arick placed his arm around Agnes.

"Don't cry, Mom," he said. "God will take care of our panther. We just need to have faith. Remember what you named my little sister."

Agnes paused. She swiped at a tear that was sliding down her cheek. She looked down at the upturned face of her son. There was no fear in his eyes. Then she looked down at the face of the daughter she had named Faith more than five years ago. There too, she saw no fright in the sparkling blue eyes that looked up at her - no fear like what she had seen the day Old Crooked Toe had saved them from the wild dogs.

"Mommy, Arick is right," her daughter said. "We've just got to believe. That's what my Sunday School teacher keeps telling us Mommy."

The little girl paused for just a second and then plugged on. "Remember, you promised some day you'd tell me why you named me Faith."

Agnes looked first into the face of Arick then Faith. Her mind calmed as she remembered the phrase she had heard so often: "The faith of a little child." Then she remembered the day her daughter was born.

"Yes," she said, "I did promise to tell you that story. It's time.

"The day you were born the doctor who delivered you could not get you breathing or your heart beating. He pronounced you dead and walked away. When the nurses saw what it did to me, they began working frantically. Soon they had you breathing and your heart beating. That was when the nurses looked at me smiling. One said, 'Look at her' as she handed me a very live little one. 'What are you going to name her?' the other nurse asked."

Agnes looked into her daughter's eyes.

"All while they were working with you I kept telling myself that I had to have faith. I said faith over and over so many times that was the only word that could come out of my mouth, Faith."

Agnes pulled both her children close.

"You are right," she said. "Both of you. I don't know what is wrong with me. I guess I was remembering how frightened we all were the day the wild dogs attacked, and what I was forgetting was the way it had all ended after I asked God to help us."

The three joined hands and hurried down the hill.

Agnes went inside and began the work she had been neglecting all day. Yet she frequently returned to the front yard and looked at the other side of the valley, to see the hunters when they came out of the woods.

Finally, she saw them.

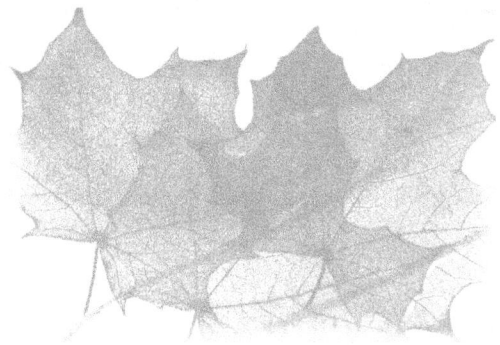

CHAPTER 14

Kennie Reeves was forking a load of hay into the barn mow when he heard the hounds. He walked out of the barn shed and listened. The baying was coming from somewhere beyond the East Hills. It sounded some distance away. Certainly it wouldn't be Old Crooked Toe way over there. He went back and finished unloading the hay.

When Kennie started back to the field for another load of hay he paused to listen. The baying of the hounds was closer now, much closer. In fact, it had to be coming from the back side of the East Hills. What could have happened over in the Blue Lick area that would send baying dogs all the way over here?

Kennie hastily unhitched the team and hurried them to their stalls. He walked out past the house where he could get a better look across the valley. That was when he saw a panther come down by Cory Long's house over on the other side of the creek. It was a big panther, much bigger than the intruder that had harassed the valley some years back. It had to be Old Crooked Toe.

Yet, what had he been doing so far east, and whose hounds were chasing him?

While Kennie was pondering the situation the old panther was splashing hastily down the creek. He was hidden from view by a rash of elderberry bushes that lined the west bank of the creek. Still, Kennie knew what the old panther was doing.

Then came the hounds, four of them, right down by Cory's house and across the creek. They were running at full speed and were several feet out in the valley before they realized they had lost the trail.

By the time the hounds found the lost scent and were singing on the trail, Old Crooked Toe was nearing the foot of the mountain. Yet the plot was not through thickening.

While Kennie was standing there trying to figure out what was going on, he saw a car racing down the road and sliding to a stop at the service station.

CHAPTER 15

A t the service station Barry Sanchez and his two friends hastily told Sam Landers what had happened, and explained why they were following the hounds.

"We knew the animal that took down a calf of that size had to be something much larger than the wildcats that have been plaguing us over at Blue Lick," Barry said. "And from what we have been reading about your panther, we reasoned that it must have been him. Did you see the animal that the hounds were chasing?"

"Yes," Sam said. "I saw the whole show."

"Are you sure that it was your panther and not some other large animal, maybe even an oversized wildcat?"

"Well," Sam began. "First of all, he isn't my panther, but I'll assure you that the critter the hounds drove across the valley was not, as you say, some other large animal, or maybe an oversized wildcat. It was Old Crooked Toe in person. I've seen him more than once and he is considerably larger than any wildcat."

"Where do you think he is headed?"

"Without question he is on his way to the Monongahela." Sam said. "Yet he may make a stop or two before he gets there. That sly old panther has many hiding places.

"If he had been angling south when he hit the mountain I would tell you to get to those cliffs atop the southern end of the mountain as fast as you could. That is where he has killed more than one dog. But he seemed to be angling north, and I'll assure you that he has his mind set on something that will be to his advantage."

"Do you think we should call the dogs in?" Barry asked. "Maybe try to keep them from getting into the Monongahela? That is a pretty big place according to my thinking."

Sam smiled. "If I know anything about hounds," he said. "There is little chance that you could call a pack of that size off of a trail as hot as that one.

"I'd say follow the baying and go as fast as you can. And if the baying of the hounds turns south, try to cut them off before they get to the cliffs.

"Yet when he crossed the valley he was angling more north. So you are probably safe there. But I don't put anything past Old Crooked Toe. Several of the folks here in the valley have been trying to put him away for many years. They haven't yet."

"Thanks," Barry said. "We not only paid a good rental fee for that pack but we posted a fifteen hundred dollar bond that we would return them in good condition. So we will sure take your advice. We don't want to forfeit that money."

The men from Blue Lick returned to their car, loaded their rifles and placed them on safety.

"Wish us luck," Barry called to Sam.

"You'll need more than luck," Sam said. "You are after a shrewd old panther that has used many tricks to stay alive over the past seven or eight years. Don't let him get to those cliffs at the south end of the mountain if you can help it."

The three set off in the wake of the hounds at a rapid pace as Sam had suggested. It seemed farther across the valley than they had thought when they looked at it from the service station. The mountain also seemed steeper than it had looked, from a distance. By the time they reached the foot of the mountain they were beginning to tire.

"With my heart condition," Juan said, "I probably should never have come along. But don't get me wrong. I'm not ready to chicken out yet."

"We'll slow up a bit," Barry said. "We can't keep up with the hounds, that's for sure. We will do the best we can and hope they bring the panther to bay before he gets too deep in the Monongahela."

"I hope they catch up with him before he gets to that big wilderness," Juan said. "Even the name of that place frightens me."

When the three reached the crest of the mountain they were winded and had to rest. They were farmers, not hound dog men. They were used to a slower life style. When they were shocking hay or hoeing corn they could set their own pace. If they tired they could go to the bucket, get a drink of water and rest for a few minutes. But this was different. They felt a need to push themselves.

"I'm beginning to think we are a bit out of our realm," Barry said. "That baying sounds pretty far away to me, and we are pretty far from home. If that panther does lead the dogs into the Monongahela we may have a hard choice to make."

"You're not suggesting that we give up?" Kandy asked.

"Oh no," Barry replied. "I don't think we have that choice. I wish we had remembered to bring the hunting horn the owner gave us when we picked up the dogs. If I had it right now I would sure try to call the pack in. The sound of that baying keeps getting farther and farther away, and we're not keeping pace."

As they started down the back side of the mountain they heard a break in the dogs baying.

"They've lost the trail," Kandy said. "That may be good for us. At least they are not racing away. It may keep the pack out of the big forest."

The break in the baying continued for several minutes. Then the hounds were singing their trail song again. But something was different. Their voice seemed louder. The baying seemed to be coming closer.

"I think they're coming this way," Juan said. "Now how would you account for that. Surely that old rascal isn't on his back trail. If he is we better get ready for him."

"Ready how?" Kandy asked.

"When we get some general direction of his course," Juan said. "We should spread out to cover a wider area in hopes that one of us could get a shot, maybe two or three. The way I'm beginning to feel I might need more shots than that if I saw a full grown panther coming at me."

The men listened.

"I'm beginning to think that won't be necessary," Barry said. "Listen close. It sounds to me like their course is heading out the mountain."

Juan agreed. "And if we are right, that panther is heading for the South point of the mountain the man at the service station told us about. He said to try to cut him off before he got there.

"Let's get back on the top of the mountain and get going before he gets a lead on us," Juan said. "Then if we are sure his course is South, we had better get a move on."

The three climbed back on top of the mountain and started walking at a fast pace, heading South. Abruptly Barry paused, cupped a hand to his ear and listened.

"They are definitely heading out the mountain below us," he said. "Let's hurry."

The three started running — Barry in the lead and Juan bringing up the rear.

They had covered less than a quarter mile when Juan dropped out. "You two keep going," he said. "With my heart condition I'm afraid I may be pushing myself too hard. I'll catch up with you later."

When the two of them had covered about a half mile they paused to catch their breath. "They're besting us," Kandy said. "And they are out ahead now."

The two began to run again, but their pace had slowed markedly. "We can't keep running like this," Barry said. "We are not hound dog men. We're farmers. Let's just keep to a fast walk and hope for the best. Those dogs are well out ahead of us and we don't know how far ahead of them the panther is."

They had walked hardly a hundred yards when the baying became more frantic.

"They've sighted him," Kandy said.

In less than a minute the baying of the hounds changed again.

"They've treed him," Kandy said. "That's their treed call."

"Thank God," Barry said as he flopped down on the ground. "Let's rest and wait for Juan to catch up. If that rascal is in a tree he's not about to jump out with those four dogs there under him."

CHAPTER 16

Old Crooked Toe knew when he heard the hounds that morning that he had made a mistake. He had come out of the thicket where he had been sleeping in one great bound and headed west, straight for Cave Creek Valley. The hounds were too close for him to fake his trail in the woods. He needed to get to the creek -- and fast. But the creek was some distance away.

To add to Old Crooked Toe's concern, he heard several voices. It was a pack that was on his trail. And the pack was followed by men with guns.

By the time the old panther had reached the crest of the East Hills and broke over toward the valley, he realized that the pack had made significant gains.

He was running hard but not at top speed. He always saved a burst of energy for a dire emergency. He hit the back of the ridge he had used the day he fought the wild dogs. As he passed the house near the foot of the hill, he saw the woman and children watching him. They were the ones he had seen the day he killed the wild dogs.

He glanced at the three of them, but only briefly.

He hit the creek with a great splash and turned down stream without a change of pace. He held close in to the bank so he could keep running rather than swimming. That way the water would hide his trail.

A little over a quarter mile down stream he crossed the creek and headed across the valley.

If he could reach the sanctuary of the woodlands before the hounds unraveled his trail, it would give him a significant lead.

He almost made it. Almost, but not quite. Still, he was well ahead of his pursuers when he started up the mountain.

By the time Old Crooked Toe reached the crest of the mountain he knew the pack had gained on him, yet he was not greatly concerned. However, he did call on that extra power he had held in reserve. He knew where he was going and he wanted to get there well ahead of the hounds. So he hurried down the other side of the mountain.

At the foot of the mountain was a small stream. It could have been labeled as a dividing line between Sugar Maple Mountain and the Monongahela.

Old Crooked Toe leaped the stream and began to climb the opposite hill. When he was about a hundred feet up he swung around to the right. That took him to a bold hump which crested a series of cliffs. These rock walls were branded "The Miniature Cliffs of Shady Creek" by those who hunted this part of the mountains.

About ten feet down the face of the cliff was a small ledge, in back of which was a small cave. That cave was the home of Bolo, a big male wildcat. Bolo had hunted the back side of Sugar Maple Mountain and deep into the Monongahela for many years. He had also, at times, plagued the farmers in the north end of Cave Creek Valley.

Old Crooked Toe knew about that den. At one time he had taken it over as one of his hideouts. But the cave had proved too small for him and he had abandoned it and moved back into the deep wilderness. When he moved out Bolo had reclaimed his retreat.

When the old panther reached the bold hump above the ledge, he ran a couple hundred feet out the mountain face. Then he turned, retraced his own trail to the crest of the cliff and leaped off onto the ledge.

Bolo was sunning on the ledge, listening to the baying hounds and feeling secure. That is, until his arch enemy landed on the ledge, almost on top of him.

If the encounter had been out in the open, Bolo might have sparred with the panther. That they had done many times. Yet because of his great size the panther had always won. If they sparred over Bolo's kill, the panther won. If they sparred over Old Crooked Toes' kill, the panther won. So Bolo's action was instantaneous -- he leaped.

Bolo landed at the base of the cliffs and was back on his feet in a second. His security was suddenly gone. There was no way he could go back to his den and the hounds were coming on strong. He did the only thing he knew to do. He ran.

He came out the base of the cliffs and headed south. He dropped down, leaped the branch, and set off along the foot of Sugar Maple Mountain.

The only safe escape the old wildcat could think of was Old Crooked Toe's hideout at the cliffs on the south end of the mountain. He had used it once before. If the hounds would spend enough time searching for the panther's lost trail he felt he could make it.

Bolo was running hard, but his ears were pointed back, listening. Matching wits with dogs was not new to him. The farmers on the north end of Cave Creek Valley had sent dogs after him a number of times. Then he had a sanctuary waiting, but not now. This was a different situation.

The hounds came down the mountain, angling north. They were running in the opposite direction from Bolo. He heard them cross the creek and sweep up the opposite mountain. Then the pack's song became broken. They had lost the panther's trail.

The broken baying told Bolo that the pack was swinging wide, searching. He had heard dogs do the same thing when he had confused his own trail in the past. He could only hope they continued their search. He knew eventually they would give up on the panther's trail. He knew also that he had left a fresh trail.

On the second wide swing the hounds failed to find panther scent. Yet, as Bolo had expected, they cut a fresh cat trail. It was similar to the trail they had followed two days ago when they treed a wildcat for the men of the Blue Lick area. At once they were singing their trail song again.

Bolo increased his speed. Yet he knew full well that he was playing a losing game. He was not a third of the way to Old Crooked Toe's sanctuary at the far end of the mountain. He knew also that the lanky, long winded creatures following him could outrun him on the long stretch, and there was a long stretch ahead of him.

Out on the back side of the mountain was an ancient gnarled oak that the timber men had left because it was not suitable for lumber or pulpwood. That tree had saved Bolo's hide once before when he was caught up in a desperate situation. Again he was desperate.

He started looking for that ancient old tree, and he found it. Found it only in the nick of time. The distance separating him and the pack had narrowed to less than a hundred feet.

When Bolo reached the tree he leaped to the lowest limb, then began to climb frantically. About half way up he stretched himself on a limb and rested for a few minutes.

Then he climbed up to where the top of the tree had blown off. It had been gone for several years and the center of the wood had rotted away until there was a slight dip. He had used that dip the other time he sheltered here. So once again he nestled down in the cavity and felt secure.

While the wildcat was visible the hounds had raged wildly. They leaped up the side of the tree. One hound even tried to climb it. He made it to the first limb before he fell back to the ground. But he did not give up. He continued to try again and again.

All the time the dogs were telling the three men at the top of the mountain that their quarry had been brought to bay. They needed help, and the three men would give them that help. But first, they needed time to rest and catch their breath.

When Juan caught up with Barry and Kandy, they talked while they rested. Then they dropped over the mountain top and started angling around the slope toward the baying dogs.

They had begun to feel jubilant. The thought of the cliffs at the south end of the mountain had vanished. They were about to take down that old panther who had eluded the residents of Cave Creek Valley for many years.

When they reached the old oak, they leaned their rifles against another tree. Then they began to circle the big Oak, looking for their quarry. Once around they went, and then again. But all they saw was limbs and leaves. No panther.

"If he's as big as they claim, I can't see where he could be hiding," Barry said. "Even if he is laying right on the part where the top is broken off, some part of him should be visible."

"Maybe the tree is hollow," Kandy said. "I see some rotted places on the stump. If he is down inside of the tree, I guess we are foiled. Then again, maybe the panther just climbed up the tree to fool the dogs, then jumped off and kept running."

"All we're coming up with is questions," Barry said. "Juan, let's hear from you. Do you have and suggestions?"

Juan shook his head and smiled. "I'm no hunter. The other day when the dogs treed that wildcat was my first hunt. I wonder, though, if the panther fooled the dogs, would it help to put one of the hounds on a lead and take him around the tree to see if he could pick up a trail?"

"That's an idea," Barry said. "Kandy, you seem to know more about dogs than me and Juan, would you try, maybe making a couple semi-circles?"

Kandy produced a lead from his pocket and selected a dog. He snapped the leash to the collar and made a close in circle, then one farther out. The hound would not put his nose to the ground so of course he did not pick up a scent. His only interest was to get back to the tree where he insisted the quarry was located.

At Kandy's suggestion the three of them made a wider circle around the tree. And they all concluded that an animal as big as the panther could not lay on the top of the broken part of the tree trunk without hanging over, even if he tried to curl up.

"We have two choices," Barry said. "We either cut that tree down, or we go home empty handed. That's how I see it."

"I'm not keen on cutting the tree," Juan said. "That is, unless we got permission from the land owner. Of course, we would need a saw and possibly some help."

"I agree," Barry said. "If you two are willing to stick with me, I'll go see what I can work out. I'm sure there is someone in the valley who has lost livestock to that panther who will help us."

Barry set off up the mountain side. He had travelled about fifty feet when he looked back and saw Bolo's back protruding above the hollow where he was hiding.

"Kandy," Barry called. "Bring my rifle and come up here. I'm pretty sure I see a part of the panther's back. He seems to be curled up in a low place in the top of the tree."

When Kandy arrived with the rifle the two men studied what they were seeing. "There must be a low place in the center where the tree broke off," Barry said. "Maybe a rotten center caused the break."

"I think you're right," Kandy said. "Now we've got to think about the dogs. If we cripple the panther and he falls down in that pack of dogs there'll be a fight. That old rascal slices up a dog or two, and there goes our fifteen hundred dollar bond out the window."

"Suppose you and Juan tie the dogs off to a tree," Barry said. "Then get your rifles and be ready in case I just cripple him. Let me know you're ready."

In a few minutes Kandy signaled that he was ready.

Barry took aim and fired. Nothing happened.

"You're too low and a little to the right," Kandy called. "I saw bark fly off of the side of the tree."

When Bolo heard the shot he reared up to see what was going on. That was when Barry took a second shot.

At the crack of the rifle Barry saw an animal leap out. For a moment the creature held to the sprouts that had come on around the break. Then it turned loose and started falling.

About half way to the ground Bolo caught a limb with his front feet and held on until the life went out of his body. Then he dropped down before two men standing with rifles ready.

Barry hurried down the hill. He was puzzled. The animal that lept out of the tree top didn't look as big as he had expected. He joined the other two. They looked at the dead animal there before them.

They looked at one another. There was shock on every face. For a moment no one spoke.

"I'll be darned," Barry finally said. "It's a common wildcat. Now how do you account for that? The man at the station vowed he had seen the hounds chasing a panther. Even said he knew it was Old Crooked Toe."

"Wait until they see three panther hunters and four well-bred hounds come packing that thing in," Kandy chuckled. "We'll be the laughing stock of the day."

"Maybe folks are right," Juan said. "Maybe Old Crooked Toe has some magical qualities. On the other hand, why would the old rascal turn himself into a wildcat just to get killed? If it wasn't so totally ridiculous I'd throw back my head and laugh out loud."

"We just as well pack up and get out of here," Barry said. "Kandy and I will divide the dogs between us and Juan, you can carry the game. I think that will be easier for you than wrestling with those dogs.

"We"ll have to keep them on leash until we get them home," Kandy said. "Then I hope we have sense enough to get them back to their owner -- and soon."

"If we had been thinking straight," Juan said. "We would have brought only one rifle with us, that would have helped some."

With the dogs on leash, rifles shouldered and game in hand, the three started climbing the back side of Sugar Maple Mountain single file. And that was how the crowd, gathered there at the service station, saw them when they emerged from the woods at the foot of the east side of the mountain.

CHAPTER 17

Kennie was puzzled. A strange pack of hounds from somewhere over beyond the East Hills chasing Old Crooked Toe. Three strangers with rifles followed the hounds across the valley and up into the mountain. He unhitched his team and put them away in their stalls. He went to the house and he and his mother discussed the situation, then decided to go and see what they could find out.

First, they picked up Pete. Then they headed to the service station to confer with Sam Landers.

Sam told them all he had learned from the Blue Lick men.

"I'm a little bit concerned about them," Sam said. "They didn't impress me as men who should be out in the wilds on the trail of a panther.

"Then they seemed to have a great concern about the Monongahela. Like it was some mysterious, dangerous place. I gave them the best advice I knew to give."

"You said one of them had lost a calf," Kennie said. "Did they seem certain that the culprit was Old Crooked Toe? It's quite a long ways over to the Blue Lick area. Did they really think the old panther had travelled that far just for a meal?"

Sam shrugged.

"They said it had to be an animal the size of the panther to have taken down a heifer, and to have torn out its throat the way it was done."

Kennie, Nancy and Pete drove back to the farm.

Kennie finished stashing his last load of hay in the barn and had just returned to the porch when they heard the baying turn into the treed sound.

Several minutes later, there was a shot, then another. Kennie looked at Pete. Nancy looked at Pete. His lips were trembling, his hands were shaking. He paused for a few seconds, then he exploded.

"I knew it," Pete almost shouted. "I just knew it. Now all is lost."

The three went inside for coffee. Then, they returned to the yard, where they could watch the foot of the mountain where the hunters would most likely appear. Soon they saw a crowd assembling at the service station.

"Let's go there," Kennie said, pointing at the station. "That will give us a grand stand seat to see the arrival of the three great panther hunters."

At the station the locals were gathering in small groups. Lemuel Long stood with three of his neighbors from the north end. The Beeler brothers were with a delegation from the south end of the valley.

Agnes Long and her two children came, but stood off to themselves. Shortly they were joined by Cory, who had left work early. Soon Bill Little and his wife joined the Long family.

Jerry Beeler left his group and joined Kennie.

"What do you think?" Jerry asked Kennie. "Has the old panther finally been brought down?"

Kennie shrugged. "I'll believe Old Crooked Toe is dead when I see his carcass lying on that concrete slab. He's been around a long time and he has outfoxed a lot of would-be executioners. Remember, that includes you."

"I can't argue with you on that," Jerry said. "But those hounds baying, then the treed bark, and then the shots. That's pretty convincing."

"It had to come sometime," Pete agreed. "I'm convinced it has come now."

Nancy listened, though she had moved slightly away. She wanted to hear what Cory and his family was saying also. She knew how Agnes felt about the panther, and she could see that Agnes was covering her eyes with her hands. Cory had his arm across her shoulders, Arick had an arm around her waist, and Faith was standing in the front facing her mother.

"It's going to be alright," she heard Cory say. "Please, honey, don't cry."

"We've just got to have faith," Arick said. "Remember what happened when the wild dogs had us cornered. This is going to turn out just as good."

Nancy moved back to her group, just as all eyes turned to the foot of the mountain. A man had emerged with a rifle on his shoulder, leading two dogs. He was closely followed by a second man leading two other dogs. The third man, keeping close to the one ahead of him, was carrying something.

Sam Landers joined Kennie's group.

"What do you reckon that third man is carrying?" Sam asked. "It sure isn't a panther. That cat would be a load for all three of them. It looks to me like he is trying to hide what he is carrying."

After a minute, Jerry said, "Maybe they cut off the panther's head as proof that they killed Old Crooked Toe. They haven't had time to skin him. Even if they had, the hide would be more than that man is carrying. What do you think, Kennie?"

"I'll just wait," Kennie said. "It won't be long now. I love mysteries, and I'm enjoying this one."

As the three hunters drew near, the sounds of the crowd drew down to a whisper, then total silence, as the men leading the dogs parted and the third man came forward. He threw his burden down on the concrete slab.

The crowd let out a collective sigh. Soon everyone was trying to talk, all at the same time.

Agnes had continued to cover her eyes. Cory drew Agnes' hands away from her eyes.

"It's time to look," he said.

"Yes, Mom," Arick said. "It's time to give thanks. Just take a look at what they brought in."

Agnes stared.

"What is that thing?" she asked Cory.

"That's a wildcat," Cory said. "That's old Bolo, the wildcat that has plagued the folks up in the north end, the one brother Lemuel has been telling us about."

Agnes bowed her head and only Cory and Arick, standing there with their arms about her, heard the soft whisper, "Thank You, God, for another miracle."

Barry Sanchez handed his dog leads to Kandy and walked over to the wildcat. He looked at Sam, who was staring in disbelief.

"Is that what you saw the hounds chasing this morning?" Barry asked.

"Absolutely not," Sam said. "What I saw was what I told you earlier. I saw Old Crooked Toe in person, and I saw four hounds chasing him."

"This is what our dogs treed," Barry said. "I shot him. And he was the only cat in that tree."

"Some folks contend that old panther has some sort of psychic powers," Sam said. "And I am inclined to think that maybe, just maybe I am beginning to be a believer.

"I'm not the only one who saw what the hounds were chasing when they passed here," Sam continued. "Here is Kennie Reeves and Pete Higgins. Then there is a lady over there that certainly knows what she saw." He pointed at Agnes. "She had a close experience with Old Crooked Toe."

Barry looked at Kennie.

"Did you see the chase this morning?"

Kennie nodded. "It was definitely Old Crooked Toe the hounds were chasing."

Barry asked: "Had you seen the panther previously?"

"Probably more times than anyone else here," Kennie said.

"I don't know why I keep asking these questions," Barry said. "I know it took a much larger animal than that one laying there to strike down my heifer and tear out her throat. I just guess the whole situation has me terribly confused.

"And you," he walked over to Agnes. "Mr. Landers said you saw the panther and the dogs."

"Yes I did," Agnes said. "They came right down by my house, maybe less than twenty feet from me and my children."

"Were you afraid?"

"Not in the least," Agnes said. "Have you been reading Bobby Cain's articles about our panther?"

"Yes," Barry said. "Over at Blue Lick, we've kept up with the history of your panther. That was why we determined at once this morning that the culprit who took down my heifer was Old Crooked Toe."

Agnes looked into Barry's eyes.

"Then you read about the panther saving some children from that pack of wild dogs which plagued our valley for so long," Agnes said. "Well, these children right here with me are the ones that Old Crooked Toe saved and I am the Agnes Long you read about."

"Indeed," Barry said as he extended his hand. "I am so glad to meet you. That article really got a lot of comment over at Blue Lick. I'd like to talk to you at length, but we've got to get these dogs back. But may I ask you a few quick questions?"

"You may ask anything you like," Agnes said.

"I'm not going to ask you if you had seen the panther before today, but," Barry smiled, "do you really believe that there was divine intervention in saving your children?"

"Do I believe I am standing here talking to you?"

"I'll take that as a yes," Barry said. "I had read the article, I just wanted to hear it from you. Now if I may ask just one more question. This incident that just happened today, do you have any explanation for it?"

"It didn't just happen," Agnes said. "It was made to happen."

"Why do you say that?" Barry asked.

"To truly answer your question, I must tell you what really went on up there at my house when my children and I were watching that panther that had befriended us, or maybe I should say saved us," Agnes said.

She began her story.

"Shortly after Old Crooked Toe raced past us, we saw four hounds hot on his trail. But that was not what caused us the most concern. Immediately after that we saw a car race in to the station. We saw three men with rifles set off after the dogs and Old Crooked Toe. That was when we became frightened.

"There was no physical way we could stop what we feared was about to happen. So I did what I had done that fateful day when the wild dogs were almost at my children. I turned to God. I bowed my head and I said 'Please, God, don't let them kill Old Crooked Toe.' -- You didn't."

"Thanks," Barry said. "You make me almost glad that we didn't kill the old panther. Now, one more question and we must go. Do you think Bobby Cain would be interested in talking to some of us over at Blue Lick about what has taken place today?"

"Bobby Cain is going to have a field day with this one," Agnes said. "And I'm certain he will be calling you tomorrow. The man who got your name and phone number just a few minutes ago is my husband. I'll be calling Bobby before the night is over."

"I'm glad to meet you," Barry said. "In fact several of the folks over my way would love to meet you and talk with you. Bobby's article about your experience really touched a lot of folks."

"Saving my children from that pack of wild dogs is not the only good thing the old panther has done," Agnes said. "I'm sure you know the story about Bobby Cain."

"No I don't," Barry said. "All I know about him is that he is the one writing those articles."

Agnes told Barry about the death of Bobby's father and how he left college to care for his mother.

"Fortunately the local paper found a place for him. His first assignment as a reporter was to go to Cave Creek Valley and dig up some information on the panther that was creating so much excitement, both good and bad.

"Old Crooked Toe took it from there. There was so much information, Bobby has had trouble keeping up with him. But in keeping up with him, and building a series of articles about him, Bobby has become a recognized reporter."

"But 'The Morning Cloak' is a very small paper," Barry said.

"Indeed it is," Agnes said. "But he is getting outside recognition. He has been asked by two of the state's largest newspapers for articles about that old panther. Now an out-of-state paper, which owns a TV station, is arranging for him to appear on a morning talk show."

Barry stood for a moment looking straight at Agnes. Then he said, "Mrs. Long, a little earlier I said that you almost you made me glad I didn't kill the panther. You have made me want to remove the 'almost.' I can stand the loss of one animal. Maybe we'll get some of that publicity over at Blue Lick that you people in the valley have been enjoying, even if we had to borrow your panther to do it.

"Now, I must go before those four dogs cramped up in the back seat of the car try to kill each other. Don't forget to call Bobby."

"I'll not forget," Agnes said.

With three men crowded into the front seat, four dogs crowded into the back seat, and a dead wildcat in the trunk, the men from Blue Lick drove away.

All the while Barry and Agnes were talking, the crowd was silent. Now there was a flurry of conversation. The main theme was, how had the old panther pulled this one off?

Agnes looked at Cory.

"The kids and I have had a very stressful day," she said. "Let's go home, get something to eat, and try to relax."

Kennie, Nancy, and Pete started to their car.

"You were right," Jerry called after him. "The old panther worked his way out of this one. Can you please tell me how?"

"I felt certain he would come up with something," Kennie said. "But I have to admit this one really floored me. Only God and that old panther know how he did it. There is one thing I do feel reasonably certain of. Old Crooked Toe is now deep in the wilds of the Monongahela."

Pete had been feeling low after he had heard the gun shots. However, he had recovered nicely when he saw the wildcat that Juan deposited on the concrete slab. He talked freely as they drove home, and accepted Nancy's invitation to stop with them and visit while she prepared the evening meal.

After dinner Kennie drove Pete home. He was still in a talking mood.

"The next time is it," he said. "The very next time is when he gets in my trap. I just tell you Kennie, his next visit to the valley is when we get him."

CHAPTER 18

Agnes was right. Bobby Cain tore into this latest episode with Old Crooked Toe like a winded and hungry fox hound tears into a juicy steak.

Bobby did call Barry Sanchez the following day. But the first person he wanted to see was Agnes Long.

"I can't tell you just how it happened," Agnes told Bobby. "But I can tell you why. It didn't just happen. It was made to happen."

Agnes then laid out for Bobby everything that had happened the previous day. Bobby was all ears. She tried to cover every detail. She explained how frightened she and her children had been when they saw the four hounds after the panther. Then there was the great fear when they saw the three men with rifles set off after the dogs and the panther. Then she told Bobby how she had asked God's help in saving Old Crooked Toe.

"You don't think that the hounds might have caught and killed Old Crooked

Toe and then just happened onto a wildcat trail?" Bobby asked.

"Not a chance," Agnes said. "If such a fight had taken place, those hounds would have been cut up pretty bad, if not killed. Some of the older folk who remember when there were several panthers around say that Old Crooked Toe is the largest panther they have ever seen.

"Also, I don't know exactly how to describe to you the speed of that old panther. I guess I could just say that when he landed on those four dogs the day he saved my children, it was just like a flash and three dogs were dead. It was not a fight, it was a slaughter.

"That old panther is alive, well, deep in that wild and wonderful land we know as The Monongahela."

"I gather you're not going to speculate on what may have taken place there in the wilderness?" Bobby said.

"To me it is just another in a series of miracles that have shrouded the life of Old Crooked Toe," Agnes said. "I like it that way and that is how I will keep it"

After Bobby finished his interview with Agnes, he went to see Sam Landers at the station. From Sam he got the names of all who had seen both the animal the hounds were chasing and the wildcat that the hunters had brought in.

"I want to talk to every one of them," Bobby said. "Not all of them today, but before I finish my article about this latest, and to me the most exciting episode concerning the old panther."

Bobby then went to see Kennie Reeves.

"I want to come back for a long talk with you some day," Bobby said to Kennie. "Right now, I thought maybe you could direct me to someone who knows the history of the area."

"My suggestion would be Pete Higgins and Dudley Newberry," Kennie said. "They're the two oldest residents of the valley. Their fathers, Gray Higgins and Jonathan Newberry were pioneers here. More than any others, they established the spirit of giving, sharing and helping that still exists today."

Bobby found Pete in his garden chopping weeds. It was a hot day and Pete was ready for a rest. So he suggested that they go to the house.

Bobby came at Pete with the same question he had asked Agnes. "Do you think that maybe the hounds caught up with the old panther, killed him and then struck a wildcat trail?"

"The dogs could never have killed Old Crooked Toe," Pete said. "He is a big cat. If they had tried to kill him he would have ripped them apart. What really happened there in the forest that day only God and Old Crooked Toe will ever know.

"Some people, as you already know, will use this incident to strengthen their belief that the old panther has some sort of psychic powers. That's fine for them, but any notion of what really happened would be only a guess."

Bobby nodded.

"Kennie said that you could probably tell me more about bears than anyone else."

"Oh yes," Pete said. "I had almost forgotten about the bears. They were such a nuisance that I don't know how I could have forgotten them.

"We couldn't stop people from throwing out garbage and I think those rascals could smell garbage for a mile. They came, some in daylight, but mostly they prowled the valley at night. They were so bad that the women and children, and some men, were afraid to go outside at night.

"Then Old Crooked Toe moved in. Pretty soon he claimed the valley as his private hunting ground. So, the bears had to go. There were a lot of fights, but that old panther is much quicker than a bear, and in a very short time the bears disappeared.

"Yessir, Old Crooked Toe scored some points with a lot of people when he drove out the bears."

"I get the feeling that, even though you built a trap to catch the panther, maybe you don't really want him killed," Bobby said.

"Funny thing," Pete said. "Sometimes I get the same feeling. I get upset with him when he does bad, like when he stole my pig right out of my barn.

"Then again, I get to thinking that, if we had killed him right away when he came, we would still be contending with the bears. The bears were constant. Old Crooked Toe is only occasional. Also, what if someone had killed him before he did away with those wild dogs that were trying to get to the Long children?"

"Then why did you build a trap? If you catch him, won't he be killed?"

"Not necessarily," Pete said. "Old Crooked Toe has always found a way out of a bad situation. He would come up with something."

Pete chuckled.

"Maybe, just maybe he would drive some kind of a deal with a wildcat again!"

"Kennie said you were one of the oldest residents here," Bobby said. "Did you grow up here?"

"Not exactly," Pete said. "I was just a small kid when my father stopped by to see his friend, Jonathan Newberry. The two of them had cut timber together for the Meeker River Lumber Company. The entire Higgins family was on its way west to become ranchers.

"Dad felt that if he didn't stop for a visit he might never see Jonathan again. So we spent two days with the Newberry family. In that time Dad fell in love with the valley and the folks here. So we stayed.

"Dad bought a tract of land and soon he and Jonathan were back in the timber business again. With crosscut saws and axes they went onto the mountain and cut logs for a cabin. They skidded them in with Jonathan's horses. They built the foundation out of native stone.

"When it came time to actually build the cabin, Dad had a 'log rollin.' That was something like a community party.

"Every able-bodied man in the valley came. In less than a day they had the walls rolled, the gable ends up and the ridgepole in place. As they went up the gable ends they laid long poles from end to end, all the way up to the ridgepole. These were the logs that the board for the roof were to be nailed to.

"At noon several of the ladies of the community came with baskets of food. As the men wolfed down their food, they admired their work and talked about other log houses they had helped build. Ours was only a one-roomed cabin. But it served us well until Dad could bring in a sawmill and have lumber milled for this house I live in now."

"How did they roof the building?" Bobby asked. "You said there were long logs for the boards to be nailed to but no rafters"

"Dad and Jonathan had made boards in the past. They were called clapboards and were made right there in the forest. What they did was find a red oak tree. One that was big, straight and with no low limbs. Red oak was used because it splits more readily than most other hardwoods.

"When the tree was down, the trunk was sawed into blocks three feet long. Each block was then split in halves, then each half was split in the middle. This process was continued, splitting every block in the middle until the two remaining pieces were thin enough to be used as a roofing board.

"The tool used to split the boards is called a froe. Trevor Phillips, who lived up in the north end at the time, brought his froe and helped make the boards.

"The interesting thing was that no money changed hands. People just helped people. The person helped wasn't expected to pay, just say thanks. In any case, he would be helping another member of the community soon.

"Since our fathers were such good friends, Dudley and I grew up like brothers. We went to school together, we attended Sunday School together, and played together.

"Dudley had a BB gun and I had a home-made bow and arrow. With those we went bear hunting up in the mountain. One day we actually encountered a real live bear. Fortunately he didn't chase us, but if he had I don't think he could have caught us. Not the way we came off of that mountain.

"We never went bear hunting again until we were old enough to hunt with a real gun and a pocket full of real live bullets.

"So you see, I had dealt with bears for quite a long time before Old Crooked Toe came on the scene and solved the bear problem."

CHAPTER 19

Bobby went the following day to see Barry Sanchez at Blue Lick. He had high hopes of finding new people and new territory for his reporting. What he found was more than he had ever hoped for.

Barry Sanchez was waiting and eager. He explained why they had four "cat hounds," as he called them, on hand when old Crooked Toe came on the scene.

"We don't have a lot of dogs here in the village," Barry explained. "What few we have are just pets. Occasionally you will find a hunting dog. Some, or maybe I should say, a few of the young folks will night hunt during the season when furs are prime. But after you go very far up that valley over on the north side you run into pretty rough territory."

"Your heifer that Old Crooked Toe killed was a special cross breed that you had hoped would add to the quality of your milk," Bobby said. "Since you run a dairy, where do you sell your milk?"

"The grocery store in the settlement is the only place I sell milk."

"Do they buy all of your milk?"

"Oh no," Barry said. "We make butter, cottage cheese and heavy cream for the community. Of course we sell it to the grocery and they take it from there."

"Certainly you must have surplus milk at times," Bobby said. "What do you do with that milk. You don't throw it away do you?"

"Johnny Snodgrass, who lives back up the hollow over there on the north side raises hogs. He takes my surplus milk. He mixes it with ground grain, mostly wheat and corn, to make a swill for his hogs when he is fattening them for the kill. There is no money exchanged between us. He gives me a sugar cured ham occasionally, or maybe a tenderloin roast when he knows my wife is preparing for company.

"Johnny does the same thing with Lilly Miller who has what we call the egg factory. She keeps white leghorn layers and furnishes the grocery all the eggs they sell. Johnny's wife may trade Lilly a pork roast for a couple dozen eggs when she is expecting company. My wife and Lilly have trades like that also, butter for eggs.

"We don't import any eggs, meat or milk products. That way we know that the chickens, the hogs and the cows are eating only good wholesome feed that is produced here in the settlement. They are not fed antibiotics or supplements to make them produce more."

"What is that big building over there?"

"That is the Church." Barry said. "Since there is only one God, and since we all worship that same God, we see no need for denominational churches. So

125

ours is just 'The Church.' It is used for worship services on Wednesday evenings and on Sundays. Any community gathering is held on the Church Lot. If it is raining or cold weather we may go inside, but that is not normal."

"You seem to have most bases covered," Bobby said. "I suppose you go to the clinic in Blue Sulphur Springs for your medical needs?"

"Sometimes," Barry said. "A few years ago Dr. Silas Baker came to us to see if we would like to have a doctor in the village. We jumped at the idea.

"Dr. Baker had retired the year before. Then he discovered that he was totally unhappy not doing what he had done all those years, because he loved it.

"Dr. Baker's father had been a doctor before him, back in the days long gone when doctors made house calls on horseback. So, Dr. Baker had bought a horse for that special purpose. He wanted the deal with us to include a stable, hay and grain for his horse.

"He sold his house in town and built his retirement home here, including a room for his office. We built him a stable for his horse and we see to the needs of his horse. We were also able to find him an old Buena Vista saddle like the one his Dad had used. He said he didn't want a cowboy saddle. He wanted to be a doctor, not a cowboy.

"Dr. Baker does not accept any type of insurance. His charges are almost incidental when compared with the present costs of medical services. If you can pay, fine. If you happen to be down and out and can't pay, you are doctored just the same.

"We have one young war widow with two small children. There is no charge to them or to the few elder couples we have with us."

"You are getting me confused," Bobby said. "And I'm sure there is much more. We haven't got to your mail service, your educational services and certainly more. How do you men keep up with everything?"

"We don't," Barry said. "Our wives do that. They have their auxiliary, as they call it. They meet regularly at the Church. There are three midwives, so there is always one to help Dr. Baker when the need arises. They keep check on folks such as the war widow I mentioned. Of course, she gets help from the Veterans Administration, but they see to it that she or her children want for nothing. They do the same thing with our two elderly and disabled couples. We have no one on welfare. We take care of our own."

"I came here to talk about Old Crooked Toe," Bobby said. "The one who got all of this started. Since we haven't got around to him, I'll come back for that another day. I can see now that I will be doing a series of pieces about your unique community, or should I call it a village?"

"We refer to Blue Sulphur Springs as our sister city." Barry said. "But of course we are not a city. Village fits the occasion better. We do have a gas station and a mail room in the back part of the grocery store."

"I'm going to run along now," Bobby said. "I want to put this information in some order while it is fresh on my mind. I'll call you and come back later for some panther talk."

CHAPTER 20

Old Crooked Toe remained away from the valley so long that some of the residents wondered if something might have really happened to him during that last chase. Their fears were fueled by the fact that four hounds had been on his trail. They felt that fending off that many dogs in a fight to death could have been difficult, even for a fighter like the old panther. Yet he was destined to let some of them know of his presence in one of his unique ways.

It was a dark night. The clouds were low and heavy and there was no moon — one of those nights when forest creatures love to travel. So travel Old Crooked Toe did.

He came out of the Monongahela, crossed Sugar Maple Mountain and padded quietly across the valley. He was now on the trail that he had used frequently, the one up past Cory Long's house. He crossed the creek, climbed up the bank and was just above Cory's house when he heard a commotion.

Old Crooked Toe was on a mission. It was a mission that was to carry him back across the East Hills and further still to the land of those who had the audacity to send four hounds on his trail. So he continued on.

Then he heard a chicken squall. That caught his attention. He paused, listened. Then another squall. Curiosity got the best of him.

So he turned out the bench above Cory's house, padding quietly, listening intently. He passed the next house and saw and heard nothing. He was directly above the widow Martha Boone's house when he heard a chicken squall again. He turned quickly down the bank until he was just above the fence that enclosed Martha's poultry lot.

There, just inside the fence, was a chicken coop. Laying close before the coop door was a wildcat. He had torn a hole in the door and was reaching his left paw through the hole, trying to snag a chicken and drag it out. He had succeeded in doing just that as the panther arrived on the scene.

Old Crooked Toe did not have to think about what to do. Of all the creatures of his forest world, he disliked the wildcat family the most. They were too small to deal him hurt, but they were the only ones that would dare to spar with him. They were quick. They would tease him to strike; then leap nimbly away.

The wildcat's jaws had hardly closed on the squalling, flopping chicken when Old Crooked Toe landed on his back. There was a single growl as the panther's great jaws closed on the opponent's head and life went swiftly from the wildcat's body.

Old Crooked Toe drew back. He heard a door slam at the house so he turned and leaped out of the pen. He paused only long enough to look back and make sure that the wildcat was dead. Then he turned back past the two houses to the trail there above Cory's house. Within minutes he was deep in the wilds of the East Hills.

He moved at a leisurely pace. There was no need to hurry. It was well past midnight when he paused on a high point above the little village of Blue Lick. He located a thicket where he could bed down, but he did not bed down just yet.

In the stillness of the night, he came down to the little creek that dropped down the north hollow past the hog farm. He entered the creek and began to follow it back up into the hills. He was a half mile up the hollow when he came to a high bluff on the west side of the creek.

This looked like a point where the wildcats that infested the rocky mountain tops might swing around for their night's hunt. So this was where he came out to check, and where he found fresh wildcat scent.

He got back in the creek, following it down to where he had entered it. He leaped off on the west side and climbed back to the high point he had selected earlier. There he bedded down for the rest of the night.

Back across the hills above Blue Lick, and farther still to the far side of the East Hills, things were coming to life in Cave Creek Valley, following a sleepless night of fear for one of it's residents.

Cory Long and his family had just sat down to breakfast the following morning when the phone rang. Cory picked up the phone and immediately recognized his neighbor's voice.

"I wondered if you might help me for a few minutes before you go to work," Martha said.

"Of course I will," Cory said. "What's up?"

"During the night I heard a commotion in my chicken lot," Martha said. "So I took my flashlight to see what was going on. I was halfway to the poultry lot when I heard a chicken squalling and a terrible growl. It frightened me so that I ran back in the house and locked the door. I didn't sleep any the rest of the night.

"I'm sorry to bother you at this early hour, but I am afraid to go out there by myself, even though it is full daylight."

"Don't you dare go out there by yourself," Cory said. "Just stay in the house and I will be right over."

When Cory started to leave, Agnes and the kids wanted to go along. So the four of them crossed the neighbor's lot and found Martha waiting at the front door.

"I just feel it was that old panther," Martha said. "And that he has eaten up all of those young chickens I was raising for fryers."

"Old Crooked Toe hasn't bothered chickens before," Cory said. "But we'll check. There can always be a first time."

They went around the house and Martha opened the gate to the poultry lot. They hurried to the coop.

"What's that thing?" Martha asked.

"That's a wildcat," Cory said. "He has a dead chicken in his mouth and he's dead. Something has killed him in the act of killing your chickens."

"Now I'm really getting confused," Martha said. "What in the world could have done that?"

"We can only guess," Cory said. "I think I know but we will probably never be sure."

"I'll bet it was that old panther, "Martha said. "And he has eaten the whole coop of chickens. Now I'll have to start all over if I'm to have any chickens to fry."

"We'll soon see," Cory said as he picked the wildcat up and threw it over the fence onto the upper side of the lot. "Now open the door."

Martha opened the door. The mother hen poked out her head, looked around, saw no predators, then came out followed by eight half-grown chicks.

"How many young chicks were there?"

"Nine," Martha said. "The only one I lost is the one in the wildcat's mouth. How do you account for that?"

"I could say it is easy to account for," Cory said. "But what I will say is only a guess. It had to be some animal larger than a wildcat to crush his head that way. My guess is that Old Crooked Toe is the one that saved your chickens. Probably we will never know for sure."

"I guess I'm lucky that the old panther just happened by," Martha said.

"Otherwise I would have had no chickens left when the wildcat got through with them."

"There is no such thing as luck," Agnes said. "It didn't just happen, it was made to happen."

While they were talking Arick had left the pen and climbed the bank up above the yard. "I think I've solved the puzzle Dad," he called down. "Come up here and take a look at these tracks."

While Agnes and Faith were climbing up to see what Arick had found, Cory turned to Martha. "I'm going to help you up the bank," he said. "I want you to see for yourself what Arick has found."

When Cory got Martha up the bank they studied the big padded prints in the soft earth. "These tracks are many times bigger than what a wildcat would make," Cory said. "Also, look at this special one. See the one toe pointing out away from the foot and there are two toes missing. Only one animal around here makes a print like that."

"Then you really think the old panther saved my chickens?" Martha asked.

"It's pretty evident," Cory said. "That crooked toe is what prompted Kennie Reeves to give the panther that name. And we all think maybe Kennie knows something about how or when or where the accident happened that crippled the old panther."

"I'll help you back down the bank," Cory said to Martha. "Then I'll have to run along so I can get to work on time. Don't you worry about the wildcat.

I will bury it when I get home from work."

"Dad, let me bury the wildcat," Arick said. "That can be my project for today."

"That will be good," Cory said. "And to you Martha, I have some good wide planks over at my place. When I get home from work this evening, Arick and I will make a new door for your chicken coop that no animal will be able to dig a hole through.

"Also, don't you ever go out alone at night when there is some disturbance," Cory said to Martha. "You can call me any time day or night when I am home and I will be right over."

Martha thanked them all and Cory and his family went back to their breakfast.

"I'll be calling Bobby Cain before the day is over," Agnes said when they were seated back at the table. "This in another of those unusual circumstances that seems to follow Old Crooked Toe."

CHAPTER 21

Back across the East Hills, and farther still to that high point above Blue Lick, Old Crooked Toe had spent a restful day. Sometime about mid-afternoon he crawled out of the thicket where he was bedded down and studied the landscape before him.

He could see sheep on the far side of the settlement, but they were too far away from the path he intended to follow after the kill. Of course there were lots of pigs close to the creek. Yet all of the pigs he had killed squealed so quickly and so loudly. They were a no-no.

Then he located a rather large calf. It was in a lot beside the pig farm and there was a plank fence between the two fields. That fence would make fine cover for an approach. The calf was near a spring house not far from the fence. It was grazing, so of course there was a good chance that it might be much farther from the fence before it bedded down for the night. That was something he would have to deal with when he got there.

Again the old panther bedded down to wait. It was a little past midnight before he began his stalk. He angled out the hill until he was well past the hog farm, turned down to the creek and stepped into it. He followed the creek down until he was near the corner where the plank fence and the hog lot fence met.

Now he paused for long minutes to look, listen and test the air currents. He found nothing that concerned him, so he began his approach.

He left the creek, leaped into the hog lot and began to slink down beside the plank fence. He was nearing the spring house before he located the calf. It had bedded down on a knoll well beyond the spring house.

If he could get over the fence without disturbing the calf, he could use the spring house as cover in his initial approach, and that he did. Now he was a good three bounds from the quarry.

He was still more than two bounds from the calf when he stepped on a twig and it snapped. The calf's head came up. Old Crooked Toe sprang into action. The calf was on its feet before he landed on it. He drove it to the ground with his great weight but it was able to get out a bellow before he could tear out its throat. He stepped back and listened.

A dog barked from the nearest house. He heard a door slam. He bellied down in the grass. The dog stopped barking. The door slammed again and he moved around to the rear of the calf that had now stopped struggling.

In the quiet of the night he tore back the hide from a rear quarter. He ate wolfishly, gulping down chunks of half chewed warm sweet meat. He was nearing a stuffed maw when the dog decided to check on what the commotion had been. When he saw what was going on, he began to bark again.

Old Crooked Toe's first thought was to chase the dog. Then he thought better of it and ran. He leaped the plank fence and loped up to the corner. He crossed the hog lot fence and followed the east side of the creek. When he neared the bold hump where he hoped to find a wildcat trail he crossed the creek, and, sure enough, he found fresh wildcat scent.

He leaped into the creek and began to wade. He was almost a half mile up the hollow when he came out on the west side of the creek. He then climbed up the rocky slope to the crest, turned south and found his way back up the hill above Blue Lick Village. He bedded down to wait for morning. He wanted to see what happened when the dogs lost his trail and picked up that of a wildcat.

CHAPTER 22

When Kandy Boder came out the following morning he yawned, stretched and gloried in the new day. The air was fresh and just a mite crisp. It made him think of impending fall.

At the barn Kandy filled a gallon bucket with the ground feed that would fatten the steer he intended to butcher come early winter

The animal was not at his feed box as he normally would have been. So Kandy walked out to the knoll above the spring house. From there he could see the entire lot, and that was when he found the carnage. He studied it briefly and hurried back to the house.

He talked briefly to his wife then went to the phone. He called his friends Barry Sanchez and Juan Wilmer. They came at once, and again the three studied a scene of carnage. Again they reasoned that the act could have been done only by an animal of Old Crooked Toe's size.

"I guess we try again," Kandy said. "Maybe it's foolish but if you both agree,

I say we go for the dogs."

"We don't have a lot of options," Barry said. "We have to try to stop him. So I'm with you on getting the dogs. But this time, let's get only a couple."

Juan agreed so Kandy and Barry set off at once for Blue Sulphur Springs where the dogs were located.

After they had the dogs Barry suggested that they drop by the newspaper office and see if Bobby Cain would like to go on a panther hunt. Of course Bobby accepted. So off they went to the settlement with a pair of hounds in their car and Bobby Cain following close behind.

While the others were gone for the dogs, Juan got his car ready. The key was already in the switch and two rifles and a box of ammunition were in the trunk. If the hounds set off toward the East Hills, the hunters would try to get around to Cave Creek Valley before the panther and the dogs got there. That way they could see for themselves what the dogs were chasing.

When both cars arrived they got the hounds out at once. They wanted to get them on the trail as soon as possible.

"What's your plan?" Bobby said. "If I'm going mountain climbing I don't want to carry a lot of equipment along."

"I would suggest that you leave your camera and anything else you have with you in your car." Juan said. "If the hounds head for the valley we will be leaving here fast."

They led the hounds out to the calf, let them pick up the scent then cut them free. They were a little surprised that the hounds did not head straight for the west hills. Instead, they leaped the plank fence into the hog lot and headed for the creek. Within minutes they were singing up the north hollow.

"I don't like this," Kandy said. "What do you think he is up to now?"

"We will soon see," Barry said. "Let's start walking up to the hill. I have a feeling we will be climbing them soon."

Now there was a break in the baying. The hounds crossed the creek a couple of times in their wide semicircles. They went again, farther up the creek and higher on the adjoining hill.

The hounds had completely lost the panther scent. So, when they cut across the fresh wildcat trail, they started singing back down the north hollow. Then they left the hollow and were bellowing out the side of the hill.

"This sounds like a repeat performance to me," Juan said. "I'm not climbing that hill until I know where they are going. The rest of you can go ahead if you want."

Old Crooked Toe, looked out from his hideout on the face of the hill. He heard the song of the hounds and felt that everything was going as planned. He even stood up in full view as the chase seemed headed to the slope below him. He wanted to hear the treed call of the hounds, followed by the sound of gun shots. Then he would climb up to the top of the hill and point his course back in the direction of the Monongahela.

Somehow the old panther knew that any further raids on the Blue Lick settlement would bring hounds. And somehow he knew that he would never hunt these hills again. Yet this chase was going as planned. Or was it?

The bawl of the running hounds should be passing below the old panther within minutes, but there was a break in their baying. Then there was a change in direction. The hounds were coming straight up the hill. Apparently the wildcat was heading for the top of the hill in an effort to turn north and head for his rocky hideout above the north hollow.

Old Crooked Toe came out of hiding and began to angle south down the side of the hill. For a brief moment he was in the open and the hunters down at the foot of the hill saw him. Then he was in cover again.

Now there was another break in the baying as the hounds overshot the wildcat's trail when it turned sharply right out across the hilltop. The lead hound came back and picked up the wildcat trail. The second hound suddenly realized that he had caught the scent of the quarry they had first been sent on. He let out a new howl that turned the first hound.

Almost at once Old Crooked Toe realized that the hounds were on his own trail, and they were not far away. He raced out the hill until he came to the trail that led to the East Hills. He came across the top of the hill and loped away. He heard the wild bellowing of the hounds when they reached his hideout and found scent that was only minutes old.

His situation was not good, but the old panther had seen worse. The idea of racing back on his own trail and leaping off to the side to confuse the hounds was not an option. His pursers were too close. If they did pop into sight and saw him they would forsake the trail and come directly at him.

If he could find a dense thicket or some outcrop to back up to he could readily fend off two hounds, but that too was not an option. The call of the hounds would bring the hunters. And he had seen the rifles that two of them carried.

Scanning the landscape out ahead, Old Crooked Toe saw a heavy clump of bushes on the right side of the trail. He raced past the bushes, leaped off to the right and circled back. He crouched down and waited.

The hounds were now running hard. The hot scent stirred the kill blood that raced through their veins.

As the hounds passed, Old Crooked Toe lunged out. They were moving so fast that he missed the first hound. He caught the second with his right front paw. Needle sharp claws ripped the dog's side from shoulder to hip.

The hound yelped with pain and fright. He leaped off to the far side of the trail, turned and raced away on his back trail.

The lead hound, realizing that he had lost the trail, turned in time to see what happened to his trail mate. He paused momentarily. That animal back there was more imposing than he had expected. He leaped wide, circled below the panther and raced after the other hound.

Old Crooked Toe stepped back into the trail. He watched the dogs disappear, then turned. He moved leisurely, pointing his course toward Cave Creek Valley.

No need to hurry now. He would find one of his favorite hiding thickets in the East Hills. He would rest until well into the night. Then he would cross the valley, find his way across Sugar Maple Mountain and, come another day, he would be deep in that wild and mythical land he called home --The Monongahela.

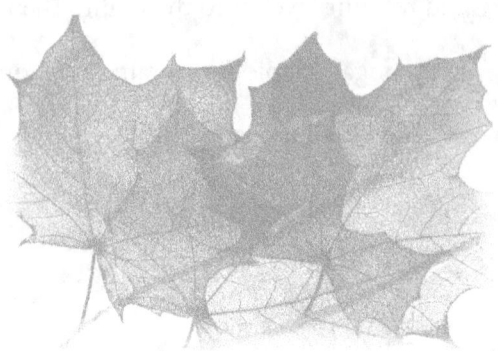

CHAPTER 23

Bobby Cain now had a new chapter in his writing career He had actually been on a panther hunt. Not just any panther hunt. An Old Crooked Toe Hunt. A hunt for the panther that had helped so much to launch him on a successful journalistic writing career.

He had visited Agnes Long after Martha Boone's experience with the old panther and her chickens. Realizing how Agnes felt about Old Crooked Toe, he wanted her to know just what had happened when he joined the hunting party. He could not tell her exactly what had taken place when the panther and the hounds came to blows. Yet, after seeing the wounded hound and seeing the two of them sneak back to the hunters, he could make an educated guess.

Bobby called Agnes and arranged to meet her at the gas station.

After their meeting, Agnes and Bobby decided they should visit Kennie and clue him in on the latest happenings concerning the panther. That led to a visit with Jerry Beeler. And, once again, Bobby discovered there was still much to learn about the old panther that had thrust him into a reporting career so suddenly. For, with each encounter, he learned something, and usually, many new things.

Once again Old Crooked Toe remained away so long that residents of the valley began to speculate on his well being. They had been told the condition of the hounds following that last encounter. Yet they could only speculate on how the old panther had fared.

Maybe, some reasoned, he had been wounded so bad that he had crawled off somewhere and died. Maybe he had been so seriously injured that he was unable to make it back to his favorite haunts in the big forest. Then perhaps he was laid up somewhere in the East Hills. Yet no search parties were sent out to look for him.

The true facts were that hunting in the Monongahela had been very good following his last brush with civilization. So the old panther had chosen to remain deep in the shadowy haunts of that mystic land where the air was always fresh and the odors of the forest were sweet to his nostrils. Yet all things, regardless of how good, change, and change they did.

Once again hunters were allowed deep into the National Forest. Once again there was massive slaughter, and, once again there was feast followed by famine.

So it was that, on a late summer evening, Old Crooked Toe once again left his land of refuge. Facing a gentle breeze that spoke of the coming fall, he crossed the little brook that separated the Monongahela from the open forest land. Like a silent shadow he drifted up the gentle slope to the southern crest of

Sugar Maple Mountain. And there, once again, in that familiar ceremony so well understood by residents of Cave Creek Valley, he announced his presence to all.

Almost a mile up the valley, on a farm that nestled close in to the foot of Sugar Maple Mountain, Pete Higgins paused to listen. He stood only a minute then sprang into action.

He laid down the hoe he had been using to dig potatoes. He picked up the bucket of potatoes and hurried into the house.

When Pete came back out of the house he was carrying his milk pail. He hobbled over to the corner of the barn. His cow was standing by her feed box, waiting to be fed and milked.

After milking the cow, Pete took care of the chickens. He fed the pig and locked it safely in the barn.

Back at the house Pete put away the milk and eggs. He put his little dog in the house and grabbed his cane. In what seemed like a very short time for a crippled old man, he had started the long walk across the valley to the residence of Kennie Reeves.

Kennie was expecting Pete. In fact he had looked out across the valley a couple times and saw him hobbling along.

"What brings you over here at this early evening hour?" Kennie said when Pete popped around the corner of the barn.

"You know what brings me over here," Pete said. "It's time to bait and set that monster of a trap out back of your barn. And this is the time it is going to work. I just feel it in my bones."

"You've had that feeling before," Kennie said. "Don't you think we should wait until Old Crooked Toe has had time to look around?"

"Quit kidding me Kennie," Pete said. "You know I'm not giving up. Not when things are just right for a catch."

After wrestling a lamb into the bait box and securing his safety, they lifted the heavy trap door and set the trigger mechanism. Then they rounded up the rest of the sheep and locked them in the barn.

"Everything looks to be in order," Pete said as he surveyed what they had done. "And I'll have you know that I did my milking and everything before I came over."

"Then it will suit you to stay for dinner," Kennie said.

Pete chuckled. "That's kinda what I had in mind," he said.

"Let's go to the house," Kennie said. "Then you and Mom can visit while she cooks up something and I do my chores."

During dinner and afterwards, Pete and Nancy intentionally avoided talking about the trap or the panther.

"I want to tell you about last Sunday," Pete said when they had finished eating. "Pam brought little Becky and her friends out. They had a great basket full of goodies and we went over to the old cabin in the sugar maples.

"I had been teaching the kids about the wild flowers. This time they brought their own flower book. They had a great time looking for new flowers to find in their book.

"Then there were the birds. We had fun trying to name the song birds when we heard them. We heard the wood thrushes. They are considered the most musical of all birds in the forest.

"The wood thrushes love big tall trees. So there are lots of them among the Sugar Maples. In the evening, just before twilight, a single thrush opened up. That set them all off and they really made the woods ring. Then, as suddenly as they started, they all stopped at the same time as twilight set in. This was the first time they had stayed for that."

"Becky and her Mom have brought you lots of pleasure," Nancy said. "But you paid a dear price. All these years with a crippled body."

"Not really," Pete said. "The good book tells us that we reap what we sow. Just look at all the joy I have reaped from that one little act of kindness."

When the conversation slowed, Kennie suggested that he drive Pete home. Again Pete avoided any conversation about the panther or the trap.

When Kennie got home he and his Mother talked briefly about some of the things they needed to attend to before winter set in. Again neither the panther nor the trap were mentioned.

CHAPTER 24

Kennie went to bed early. He was awake for a time but when he fell asleep he rested well. Like the last time that he had felt that the big decision might be eminent, he had made up his mind not to worry, just to let events take their course.

Early the next morning, while Kennie and Nancy were having their first cup of coffee, there was a loud knock on the door.

Kennie went to the door and opened it. There stood Pete.

"Come in Pete," Kennie said.

Pete did not move. His face was white. Both of his hands rested on his cane and they were trembling. He looked like something terrible had happened.

"What's the problem, Pete?" Kennie asked.

"We caught him," Pete blurted out.

"That's good," Kennie said. "Come on in and let's talk about it."

"That isn't good," Pete said. "All my life I've tried to help people, never to hurt them. Now I've done something that will hurt my best friend. That was the last thing I would ever want to do."

Nancy came over. She placed an arm about his crippled old shoulders. She led Pete in and seated him on a chair.

"Now," she said, "let's get ourselves calmed down. This isn't the end of the world. We will just give things time to work out."

"I don't like the way things are going to work out, Nancy," Pete said. "All I was thinking about was myself. I wanted my trap to be a success. Then I could say at least one of my ideas hadn't been a failure.

"Look what I've done! Now Kennie will have to make a decision that he doesn't want to make. Then he will likely have to do something to the old panther that he doesn't want to do."

"Wait Pete," Kennie said. "You are not making sense. We set the trap to catch the panther. So what is the problem?"

"The problem is that when I saw Old Crooked Toe in the trap, I realized that I didn't really want to catch him.

"My first decision was to open the trap door and let him out. When I tried to lift the door with these old muscles I couldn't. Then I thought you might help me lift the door and let the panther go."

"Hold it," Kennie said. "Now let me tell you something. What you have done is probably the best thing that could happen to me.

"Another two months and it will be exactly eight years since Old Crooked

Toe and I first met.

"What happened that night there on the back side of Sugar Maple Mountain was hard for even me to believe. Since many people do not believe in modern day miracles I felt most folks would not believe me if I told the full story. So at first I hesitated to tell it even to my own mother.

"All these years I have kept to myself the happenings of that night. The longer I kept it to myself the less I wanted to talk about it. So it has just drug on. Now, even my closest friends, even Katie, have begun to wonder about me. So it's best I get it over, put it all behind me."

"But," Pete said. "But maybe you just might ... You know what I am trying to say and I don't know how to say it."

"Yes, I know Pete," Kennie said. "We'll just let the chips fall as they may. Everything will work out and the sun will come up again tomorrow.

"As for today, I'm going to need support from you and Mom and Katie. Lots of support. So get yourself together and get ready to help me.

"What I'm going to suggest is that you and Mom visit while she gets breakfast and I do my chores."

Kennie turned to Nancy.

"Mom," he said, "would you call Katie for me? Tell her what has happened and ask her not to tell anyone until she can come over here and we make our plans for the day. Also ask her to bring Bobby Cain's phone number with her.

"Fortunately this is Saturday and Katie doesn't have to work. Tell her to go ahead and have breakfast first, then come as soon as it is convenient."

When Kennie had taken his milk pail and headed for the barn, Nancy and Pete watched from the kitchen window. They saw the cow by her feed box, waiting to be fed and milked.

Much to their surprise, Kennie did not head out back of the barn where the trap was located. Rather, he fed the cow and began milking.

Nancy started breakfast while Pete continued to watch Kennie. When Kennie had finished milking he set the milk pail on the little shelf pegged into the side of the barn. He went to the cellar house where the deep freeze was located. When he came out he was carrying two wrapped packages, one in each hand.

He now headed out back of the barn where the trap was located. He was gone several minutes. When he came back, he finished his chores, got the milk pail and headed for the house.

They had finished breakfast when Katie arrived.

When Nancy let Katie in the door she was visibly upset. Without saying a word she ran to Kennie and grabbed him. She held on, sobbing softly.

Kennie held her close for a few seconds, then pushed her back.

"Where is my brave girl?" he asked. "Get yourself together. I'm going to need your help today. Lots of help. Maybe the most support I will need from you in a long, long time."

"I'm sorry," Katie said. "It just hit me while I was driving here that you might . . . Well . . . have to do something I feel maybe you don't want to do. It's all been a mystery. In fact, I don't even know what to think."

"It's not going to be a mystery for much longer," Kennie said. "I know it is something I should have cleared up a long time ago. I think after today we will all be better off. But today I am going to need all the support I can get, and -- I will be counting heavily on you."

"I'll not let you down," Katie said. "Sometimes I'm a bit emotional. I'm sure you know that by now."

"Do you have Bobby Cain's phone number?"

"I not only have his number with me but I have already alerted him. He's expecting a call."

"Would you call him and see if he can get here by eleven this morning. I want to be sure of that before we make our plans."

Katie went to the phone. After her call, she returned to them.

"He said he was ready. Assured me that he will be here on time," she reported.

"Now there are others that I want present," Kennie said. "And, I hope you will help me get them here."

"I'll do anything you ask," Katie said.

"Of course there will be Mom, Pete you and me," Kennie said. "And I want you to bring your Dad. The only others that I want present are Jerry Beeler, Agnes and Cory Long, and the Long children if they want to bring them.

"Now if you are wondering about my selection, I only want those present who I feel sure will believe me. Getting the story out to the rest of the community

I will leave up to Bobby Cain. He always does a great job with news, so I know I can count on him."

"What part of it do you want me to do?" Katie asked.

"When you pick up your Dad," Kennie said. "Would you mind driving on out and tell Jerry? Emphasize to him that he is to come alone. Then would you contact the Longs with the same message?

"Now again," Kennie said. "The only ones I am having outside of family have openly expressed a belief in miracles. And, the experience I am going to relate to you this morning is, in my humble opinion, a miracle."

"I had better get going," Katie said. "Since Cory doesn't work on Saturday, I had best catch him before the family makes other plans. Then it will give Jerry a little time to change any plans he might have."

When Katie had left, Kennie turned to Nancy.

"Mom," he said, "Would you drive over to Joe's Place and order some hot dogs, hamburgers, drinks, and fries? Have him deliver it at twelve o'clock."

Kennie knew it was going to be a long morning. He asked Pete to help him get his long ladder from the barn and bring it to the house.

"I'm going to do some painting on the gable ends of the house," he told Pete.

When they went back in the house Kennie said. "Pete you know where the coffee is. Make us a fresh pot of coffee and we will have a cup or two before everyone gets here. I have an item or two to take care of."

When Pete busied himself with the coffee maker, Kennie went to his room.

He loaded his shotgun with a pumpkin ball. Then, he got the plastic rolled item from under the bed and slipped out the back door, taking everything to the trap. He placed the items on top of the trap and hurried back to the house.

Two cups of coffee later, Kennie felt he was ready to do what needed to be done.

CHAPTER 25

It was a somber group that trekked from the house, out past the barn and to the trap. Everyone had arrived on time. Katie had emphasized eleven o'clock and that was when they all came. There was little conversation, and that was mostly whispered.

When they reached the trap they found Old Crooked Toe laying calmly in the center of the trap. He was not fighting the enclosure as one might have expected him to do. He gave no heed to those who gathered around him.

Katie came and stood by Kennie. Everyone gathered around the trap.

Cory and his family stood a little apart in their familiar family pattern. Cory held his right arm around Agnes, his left arm around Arick, and Faith stood in front.

When Agnes saw the gun laying there on the trap she bowed her head. Only Cory and Arick heard the soft whispered prayer: "Please, God, don't let him kill Old Crooked Toe."

"I'm going to tell you an experience I had nearly eight years ago," Kennie began. "In fact if this gathering had happened three months later, it would have been exactly eight years since this old panther here in the trap and I had our first meeting.

"The Blue Sulphur Springs Veneering Company owned a tract of land on the back side of Sugar Maple Mountain. On that land were eight wild cherry trees that had reached sufficient size for veneering. They wanted those trees cut and the butt log skidded out to where their truck could get to them. I got the job.

"Since they wanted the trees cut when the sap was down, I had waited until late fall. I had been cutting over a period of days. It was a work that I was enjoying so I had not rushed through it.

"I would cut one tree at a time, edge the bark at the drag end and Prince would drag the log to the top of the mountain. I had to use chains for dragging since the company did not want grabs driven into the wood. They were not old trees and the logs were usually around six to eight feet long. That made a log that Prince could handle well.

"On this particular evening I was cutting the last tree. I had worked late because I was trying to get finished.

"The weather man had talked of a series of early winter storms he was expecting. Now I could see, by the clouds and the wind, that one of those storms was very near. I wanted to beat that weather.

"I had that last tree almost down when I paused to rest and straighten myself.

The owner wanted the trees cut close to the ground so it was a bit tiring.

"I was about ready to get back to my saw when I heard a strange cry. At first I thought it sounded like a baby in distress. Of course it could not be that here in the deep backwoods. It had to be some animal.

"My first thought was to get the tree down and get out of there. But when I heard the second, then the third cry, I decided to check.

"The tree I was cutting was on the edge of a shallow ravine. It was fairly open for a space but ended in a wall of tumbled boulders. I went to the place where the cry seemed to come from, parted the weeds and brush, and found myself facing a rather large panther.

"I didn't jump back in fright, because I saw no menace in the cat. His ears were erect, his lips did not curl. His eyes did not narrow. It was more like the meeting of a couple of old friends -- maybe. Then I saw why he did not run away at my approach.

"Apparently he had been sleeping there in the ravine when I started cutting the tree. Rather than come back down the ravine past me, he had attempted to climb out over the boulders at the upper end. I reasoned that he had pulled on one of the boulders in climbing so that it rocked up and then slid back, catching his left rear foot under the lower end and his left front foot under the upper end.

"I could see nothing I could do so I started back to my saw. Then I stopped. If I left the panther there he might suffer a slow death. If I would have had my rifle I probably would have shot him. But of course I did not have a gun with me.

"I went back and took another look. I could see where I might get my hand spike under the middle of the boulder. Maybe then I could rock it up enough to free both feet of the panther.

"Now a hand spike is a simple tool we timber men make right there in the woods. We select a small sapling about four or five inches across at the butt and two to three inches some five to six feet up. We cut it there, then slant the heavy end so that it can be used to slide under a log to move it or to raise it to get a chain under it.

"Armed with my hand spike I lowered myself into the ravine. I moved slowly, trying not to alarm the panther. Yet nothing I did seemed to bother him. His expression never changed. I was just starting to ease the hand spike in place when the storm struck.

"There were two things that I had not taken time to consider. One, that I was working within the fall space of the tree I was cutting. The other, how near the tree was off.

"First came the wind, a powerful gust that sent the tree crashing down on both me and the panther. The little top limbs of the tree knocked me face down on the ground.

"I had been hit so hard that it took me a few minutes to realize what had happened. Then slowly I began to comprehend my predicament.

"Moving as carefully as I could, I turned my head until I could see the panther. That was when I got another shock. The tree had knocked me so close to the panther that, if he was so minded, he could reach my face with his right free forearm. I lay very still, trying to reason what to do.

"My first impulse was to try to move my upper body away from the panther. That I could only do by sliding back under the little limbs that were all over me. To do this, I would have to find a way to lift some of the limbs.

"When I tried to move my body I found that something had my right leg pinned to the ground. In fact, it had me so fouled that I could not move my body without causing severe pain to my leg.

"I reasoned that if I could determine what was holding my leg I might be able to work the hand spike under the limb that had me pinned. But I soon learned that such was impossible. I was simply pinned to the ground and that was it.

"I wanted to cry out for help, but that would alarm the panther. He had twice emitted that simple cry of his, so I decided to try. In a very low voice I spoke the word, help. It seemed not to bother the panther. So I continued, spacing the calls, and growing louder each time. Yet, even as I called I realized how futile it was.

"My voice would have to travel up the back side of the mountain, then down the other side and out into the valley for someone to hear it. That, of course, I knew was impossible. On the other side was the Monongahela.

"My only hope was that some hunter might still be in the woodlands somewhere. That too was most unlikely. The storm was not just brewing, it was already here. Yet I called, over and, over again. Called until I was too hoarse to call.

"In a situation such as mine was then, time seems to tick away very slowly.

"The wind continued in heavy gusts. Then came the rain. It simply poured. Within seconds it seemed, both of us were soaked. A better word might be drenched.

"That storm cloud passed. It lightened up. Then came more clouds, each seemingly loaded with water they wanted to rid themselves of, and we were right there to share it all. So many individual showers that I lost count. Or, maybe I wasn't counting.

"Through it all our eyes held. We might say it was as though each was watching to see there were no aggressive acts by the other. But I don't think that was the case. I believe each were looking for help from the other -- help that never came.

"Long minutes turned to long hours. I began to feel faint at times. The showers had stopped, but a snow squall dumped a blanket of white on both of us. Fortunately it was warm enough that the snow soon melted. Yet it served to further cool the air until there was a real chill in it.

"Eventually the clouds broke. When there was a clear place we discovered that there was a full moon. It was during one of those breaks in the clouds that I got an idea.

"I had gotten the hand spike almost under the rock holding the panther prisoner when the tree came down. If I could slide it a little farther I might be able to rock the boulder back toward me so that it would free the panther.

If that worked it would free me from the constant fear that the big cat might eventually be a menace.

"To do what I planned would require that I get my right arm back under me so that I could lift my upper body enough that I could have some leverage with my left arm and hand. This required a bit of effort because of the weight of the mass of little limbs on my back.

"It took several minutes to get in a position where I could have some movement with my left arm. Then I felt any visible action on my part might disturb the panther. Knowing exactly what to do was like playing a shell game. So I waited several minutes before I began to put pressure on the hand spike.

"While I waited, another series of clouds shut out the moon. Still I hesitated until those clouds passed and I could see the panther clearly. Then I moved, ever so slowly -- a fraction of an inch at a time. Minutes passed. Still no movement of the boulder.

"Then it happened. The boulder rocked toward me. The sudden movement of the boulder caught the panther's attention. His head jerked up. For a moment I felt a flash of fear. Yet his ears stayed erect, his lips never curled and his eyes never narrowed.

"Almost at once he jerked his left front foot and found it free. Then he pulled up his rear left foot. His expression changed. He knew he was free. And I had the feeling that the panther knew I was the one that had released him. Yet for a moment I felt a new tinge of fear.

"Maybe he had been trapped for longer than I had thought. Maybe he was hungry. If so, there was a meal right before him.

"That was when the clouds came again and this time with a furious little shower. When that moved on and the moon came back out there was no panther. I imagined I had heard him go. Yet with the wind rustling in the tree limbs overhead there was no way I could have heard the soft fall of his furry pads.

"Now, much to my amazement, I had a new feeling of aloneness. For just a flash I regretted releasing the panther. But it was only a flicker. Yet, why did I feel more alone? -- Because I was more alone.

"It was now well into the night. I was very cold. My leg pain had increased with every movement of my body. I was beginning to wonder whether I could make it through the night. Surely tomorrow a search party would come looking for me. But would they know where to look? And, would I still be alive?

"I found myself fading away. It frightened me. If I passed out, would I ever recover? If I went to sleep, would I ever awaken?

"I now felt more free to move or to raise my voice. So I tried calling again. But the sound that come out was terribly weak. I tried moving my body so I could see what held my leg. That too failed. I was simply trapped. That was when my mind went back to family history to find some situation comparable to the one I now found myself in. And that was when I remembered what my family referred to as the 'Miracle of Grandpa Henchman' ...

"The episode concerning Grandpa had taken place long before my time, yet

I had heard it repeated more than once. Grandpa, according to the story, had taken a terrible fall. He was so badly broken up, that, after weeks of treatment, the doctors had given up hope of any recovery.

"According to the story, Great Grandma Samantha had never given up hope. She had continued to pray. She continued to insist that Grandpa would recover. He did recover and lived a normal life. That was why they called it the Miracle of Grandpa Henchman.

"Did I believe in Miracles? I had never thought on it. I had never prayed. I had never asked anyone for anything. I had never asked God for anything. My mother used to tell stories about how fiercely independent I had been, even as a small child.

"Without reasoning, without any thought or planning, I suddenly heard my weak voice say, 'Please God, help me.' At once a wave of hope seemed to flash through my entire being. I called for help a second and then a third. With each call my voice sounded stronger, my hope greater.

"With my fifth call for help I thought I felt movement of the limb holding my leg. Was it real, or was it my imagination? I hesitated. Then I called again.

"With that sixth call I was sure I felt movement of the limb. I jerked my leg. It came out. I was free. It was a miracle. I was elated. And that was when I made one of, if not the greatest, mistake of my life. I forgot to pause and thank God. Of course I did later, many times.

"My elation did not last long. When my foot came out from under the limb

I felt it fall to the side. The pain seemed to double. That was when I knew my leg was broken. I was very cold, terribly weak, completely soaked and I was far from home.

"I was, of course, already face down. So I raised myself onto my hands and knees and began working myself out from under the little limbs that covered my body.

"When I was free of the limbs, I decided to crawl up around the crown of the tree. Dragging my broken leg over those little limbs had proven very painful. Getting up the bank out of the ravine was an obstacle, but I made it. I was now on the way home.

"I didn't crawl fast. I was weak. But I was crawling. Then I had a terrible thought. Horses have a great fear of large cats. If the panther came out of the ravine on the mountain side and passed Prince, he had probably broken free and was long gone. But when another spate of clouds passed and the moon came out again, I could see my faithful old horse still standing there waiting for me.

"When I reached Prince, I had a problem getting up on my good foot. Why the horse knelt down, I did not know. He had never been trained to do so. But he kneeled down on his left knee and I grabbed the brass knob on top of the left hame with both hands. When Prince raised back up he lifted me onto my good foot.

"I locked my right arm about the hame of the harness, unsnapped the lead, that had kept him tied, with my left hand and spoke softly to Prince. He seemed to understand the situation and walked ever so gently.

"Prince kept turning his head about trying to see me, but the blind of the bridle was in his way. I had him stop, unbuckled the throat latch and slid the bridle off of his head. I hung it on the hame and we were walking again. Now he constantly checked, first me then the trail.

"It was a long climb up the mountain. My problem was having to swing my body uphill since I could use only one leg.

"At the top of the mountain I had Prince stop. Holding to the brass knob with my left hand, I withdrew my right arm from about the hame. I shook it, exercised it and got the blood flowing. Then we were on our way down. This was much easier. I could swing myself in longer hops so Prince speeded up.

"We were nearing the end of the skid road when we saw a light bobbing out ahead. That turned out to be Dad. He had lit the old oil lantern and was coming to find me.

"Dad was already exhausted. With the present condition of his heart he should not have been out of the house, much less trying to climb the mountain. I had him set the lantern down and lock his left arm around Prince's right hame. With one clinging on either side, Prince carried us right up to the back porch.

"Somehow Mom got Dad onto the porch and inside the house before he got completely down. Then she came running with a chair for me to use as a crutch. With it she got me into the house and onto the couch.

"Mom then ran to the phone and called Pete Higgins. That was before Pete got broken up saving the life of a child. Back then Pete was the one in the valley that everyone called on for help.

"Mom and I talked about that night later. We knew that as fast as Pete got there he had to run all the way across the valley.

"While Pete was coming Mom had called Doctor Shields and told him what was going on.

"When Pete arrived he helped Mom get Dad up and to bed. Then he took care of the faithful old horse who was still waiting at the back porch for me to come.

"The first thing Doctor Shields did when he arrived was to give me a shot. While the shot was taking affect he worked with Dad, stabilizing him.

"After the shot took affect I didn't know a lot of what was going on. But I was to learn later that, with the help of Mom and Pete, Doctor Shields cut off my pants, got the shoe and sock out of the way and set and splinted my leg.

"Pete stayed with Mom the rest of the night and did my milking and feeding before he went home. Later that day both he and Mollie came back to help Mom. And Pete continued to come and do my chores until I was able to get about.

"We know that all mortals as well as all animal life belongs to God. We are all His to use as He sees fit. I had a feeling I knew what had taken place there in the ravine that fateful night. But I needed to be sure.

"So it was that I had Mom take me to Doctor Shields' Clinic and have him put a walking cast on my broken leg. Then I saddled Prince and he carried me back across the mountain to the ravine in question.

"My saw and axe were still there just where I had left them -- A little rusted but still useable. So I took them with me and entered the ravine. I didn't want to have to fight my way through those limbs again, so I chopped me a path.

"When I reached the rock that had held the panther prisoner, I saw two small objects laying just below the rock. I picked them up. They were two toes the rock had ground off of his left rear foot when the foot was mangled. I put them in my shirt pocket. Now Mom knows what those two strange objects in the dish there on the table beside my bed is. But that was not what I had come to see.

"I now chopped my way in to the limb that had held my leg. And there I saw what I had expected to see, tooth marks on the green bark of the limb. When I examined it carefully, I found a broken tooth embedded in the bark.

"I grasped the limb with my right hand and attempted to lift it. I couldn't budge it. I lay my axe down and tried with both hands. Still not the slightest movement. Some source, greater than any available to mankind, had given the panther the strength to lift that limb.

"I got my saw and cut off a two foot piece of the limb. When I examined the under side of the limb I again found tooth marks. When I got it out into the bright sunlight I found another broken tooth embedded in the bark. I brought that piece of limb home, wrapped it in plastic and hid it under my bed. It is in that piece of plastic there for anyone who wants to see it

"That is my story," Kennie said. "And now if I do that which I need to do I will have to do it quickly, or I will fail again."

He grabbed up the gun, took aim at the old panther's head.

CHAPTER 26

As Kennie squeezed the trigger an arm shot out and drove the gun barrel up so that it exploded in empty air. Kennie lowered the gun. The barrel felt warm to his cold and sweaty hand. He turned his puzzled eyes on Katie.

"Why did you do that?" he said.

"That old panther saved you for me," she said. "I saved him for you."

Kennie looked around the half circle. He didn't think he saw a dry eye. Both Agnes and Faith were crying softly.

No one spoke.

Pete hobbled over to the trap. He pulled the wooden pin that locked the trap door in place and threw it far out into the field, then backed away.

Jerry Beeler came over to one side of the trap, Cory Long to the other side. Together they lifted the heavy trap door and laid it to the side. Then they both backed away.

Old Crooked Toe, who had flattened down when he heard the gun blast over his head, now raised up. He shook his head and began to walk slowly out of the trap. When his body was about two thirds of the way out he paused.

He seemed totally oblivious to those about him. He turned his head and for brief moments his eyes met those of Kennie. They held just as they had held on that fateful night now so near eight years ago. What message passed between them, only God would ever know.

He took two more steps, paused briefly and looked at Agnes. For only seconds their eyes met, just as they had that day when he killed the wild dogs and saved her children.

Then he assumed that regal pose, and why not. After all he was still the King of the Monongahela. He walked slowly, deliberately. He did not hurry. He did not look back. When he was a good hundred yards away he began that gentle rolling lope that carried him swiftly across the valley.

To Kennie, watching his friend go, it seemed that the bright noon day sun turned his tawny coat to pure gold that flashed and glittered as he loped.

Then the woodlands seemed to open and swallow him up. And Old Crooked Toe was gone from Cave Creek Valley.

Only Katie, standing there with her arm around Kennie's waist, heard the soft whisper, "Thank You ,God, for another miracle."

Other books by this author:

The Pecos Trail

Tales of the Deep Woods

The Long Road

Spirit of a Dog

The Music of Home

www.ingramcontent.com/pod-product-compliance
Lightning Source LLC
Chambersburg PA
CBHW071247130626
46556CB00003B/1205